BLACK
COAT
DAY

BLACK COAT DAY

FRANK PENDLEBURY

To order additional copies of this book, contact:
Xlibris
UK TFN: 0800 0148620 (Toll Free inside the UK)
UK Local: 02036 956328 (+44 20 3695 6328 from outside the UK)
www.Xlibrispublishing.co.uk
Orders@Xlibrispublishing.co.uk
756535

CONTENTS

Prelude ix
Inspiration...xi
The Selection Process xiii
On the Line.. xvii

PART ONE

The Slob...1
A Perfect Dozen 3
Overly Encompassed..4
Gasbag Garrotted 7
Blind Ignorance 10
The Scruff...12
The Poseur 19
Paper Tiger 24
Grip..28
Necrotic Neglect..32
Women, Cricket & Golf 34
The Crook...36
Selfish Silverfish..38
Wild Foul...42
London Calling.. 48
The Mouth 50
Violence to Order 56
Digging for Guilt...58
Either Way 64

PART TWO

Covert Communications 71
Who's Who? 78
Alias Entanglements 81
Two for One 85
Compelled 87
Closet Case 91
Birds of a Feather 93
Stone Cold 97
Star-Crossed 102
Strictly Business 106
New Year 112
Grave Encounter 115
On the Scent 120
Killing Glee 124
Death of the Apostate 135
Strange Week 142
Hidden Hands 147

PART THREE

My War 153
The Professional 164
Sworn 166
Salvation Sans Redemption 184
Two of a kind 194

For Mary

PRELUDE

Primary Phases

M urder provides a unique pleasure. For those of us with the necessary disposition. Ending another human life affords sensations which stretch adequate description. Gratifying deep, primordial stirrings well beyond the experience of generality. Still, for many years, this truth escaped my perceptions. Delusion beguiled motivation.

At the time, my slayings were all noble acts. Essential service. This fallacy kept me ignorant of the brutish fiend residing within my mind. The hidden entity pulling the strings. Although, I remained fully conscious of all my dire deeds, despite this dank influence. And as much blood is on my hands, none of my quarry were innocent. Feeling then and now the World needed me to remove those people from existence.

Yet my methods cannot be defended. For my Targets were slain in barbaric, inhuman ways. Only savagery and bloodlust delivered with terrifying indifference could sate my monstrous alter-ego. Often, my thoughts became philosophical. Seeking fresh perspective on these covert activities, my life's secret work. My murderous cravings. A lonely path chosen in complete, lucid consciousness. Castigating callous judgement on each chosen Target. For justice? Or to satisfy a raving, unbridled bloodlust? The answer is an unpalatable truth. An undisciplined, unacknowledged veracity which haunted my life for many years. Releasing a deeper urge. A desire for absolute self-governance, growing from within to fight against these stygian desires. To stop me. To save me.

INSPIRATION

Many hours of my youth were spent reading. In particular, very old books. Reading the history books gave me greatest pleasure. To learn about the remarkable characters of times past. Their struggles and achievements.

One distinct tale struck a chord in me. It told of emissaries from Europe, seeking an audience at the court of Genghis Khan. Ruler of the all-conquering Mongol Hordes, rampaging westwards across Asia into Europe during the early thirteenth century. The Pope and Holy Roman Emperor sent heralds to the man behind the irresistible military power which had erupted from the Steppe. Their message explained how the Pope, God's Shepherd upon Earth, ruled over all secular monarchs in Europe. Implying only heathens and God-less barbarians denied his Holiness the Pope spiritual dominion over their lands. After heeding their message with prodigious serenity by way of his interpreters, the Khan of Khans told them;

"Go home and tell your leaders that I am the Wrath of God upon the Earth, to resist my power is futile. All who refuse to kneel before me, shall be destroyed."

This episode made an indelible impression. Those words were taken to heart and made my own. The decision to become a vigilante, after over a decade of active military service befell me. Armed service overseas had rewarded me with the craft of taking lives as well as the discipline and patience of specialised soldiery. Possessing the persistence and attention to detail necessary to perform my adopted special duties without being detected.

Those who were chosen to be targeted were not obvious, or popular choices. The rapists, violent burglars and casual murderers. Nor the gangsters selling bad news and misery up and down the land, corrupting the youth and staining our towns and cities with their filth. Or child-abductors, molesters and their ilk. All too obvious. Although the temptation to exterminate a few of those damned enough to fall into any of the above categories did overwhelm me, on occasion. This urge would become irresistible, transmuting into an ungovernable force, screaming for justice. Less said about those eliminations, the better.

———◇———

Remaining free, motivated my choice of Target above all other factors. To leave no trace of a pattern for murder detectives to follow. The Targets were complex. All different characters. Each of them guilty of causing death and misery by their neglect, greed or indifference, to numerous families. Some I sensed buried the guilt, deep in their dark hearts. Others, possessing no troubling morals, felt little remorse for the lives they'd cut off, despite having caused so much grief and sorrow. Taking little pleasure in ending their lives. Doing God's dirty work was reward enough. That's how I liked to think, at the time. This Secret Service of mine had divine approval and had been ordained only for me to undertake.

THE SELECTION PROCESS

Seeking and stalking each Target brought satisfaction. To learn of their habits. Figuring out how to get to them undetected. Then the planning and fine-tuning. The details. The death, could be exciting, in the moment. Yet no enduring gratification derived from it. My thoughts at the time were with the victims of the Target. Those feelings giving my heart fibre to carry out the dirty task. Kill the Target, clear the decks, move on.

My processes involved moving to a large town or city. Acquiring knowledge of death through neglect cases by accessing local news archives in central libraries. Many potential Targets were available, at face value. Plenty of people could be blamed for all kinds of death and injury. Yet I had to be specific. Seeking those whose choices and behaviour had rendered the fatal occurrences inevitable. Somehow flawed character put blood on their hands. A flaw so deep it left them shameless, unrepentant. Whenever a feeling told me who the next Target should be, I knew with absolute conviction. Each and every time.

'Kill him.'

A bell struck deep in the heart. Manifest Destiny. A calling. A Duty to fulfil. It first became a matter of gathering information on the Target. Their private life, affiliations, business practices. Once enough reliable information could be utilised, the planning process began.

First; - *'How to kill them?'*

Then; - *'Where to do it?'*

Followed by the most pertinent query of all; - *'When?'*

All this used up a lot of time. And, for a while, my methods were sound. However, as time went on, my murders took on a primal theme. I stopped counting after several dozen. It seemed egotistical to keep count. Numerous Target eliminations, sundry other slayings, armed conflict, both legal and illegal, each add their count to my tally of death. Murder, some would call it. Although the deliberate homicides carried out by my hand could be called justice, writing this so many years later, motives have since become less convincing than conscience. Perhaps I'd sought vengeance on behalf of these people's victims, or perhaps I just needed a good enough reason to kill.

One desirable option for a professional is to cause the murder to appear to be an accident. Yet for me, such methods were too detached. Preferring to be close enough to ensure death did occur. Close, sudden and fast. Pistols would be best for this type of hit, but my favourite preferences, well, let's say the hands-on approach appealed to me.

Asphyxiation or blades were most effective for the quick, abrupt kill. At night, when the Target would be alone, often the worse for wear from booze and other indulgences. This provided the cover of dark to operate in and make good my escape. It often meant the body remained undiscovered for many hours. Sometimes even days or weeks. A bonus. By then I'd be long gone.

However, I have my own shortcomings. Weak, fraught with sin. On occasion, after researching and following an individual for months, indifference hardened into vengeful hatred. As if it were my own loved ones lost to the Target's failings. An irresistible yearning grew in me for these bastards to acknowledge their homicide before succumbing to it. To know they were being murdered. Not just to die. They had to suffer.

Each of them had a number of enemies. From more bad deeds, hidden in the closets of their minds. Some of them would not have known who to blame for their own grim demise. This fact kept my activities anonymous. Being unknown to the Target kept me incognito. Logic suggested any investigation would become mired down in the intrigues of their own sordid life. Their known enemies would pass all questioning and enquiries, all alibies being genuine.

The local police would file the case as unsolved and most likely move on. The Target would become just another statistic.

I acted alone. No one paid me to kill these individuals. No one had to, having neither need nor desire for such payment. Taking on the work under my own volition. My Secret Service to the World. My way of giving something back, with God my sole witness. Although adhering to no strict faith nor religion, my relationship with Creation remained constant and untainted.

With regret, I couldn't kill them all. Selecting who to target in a land of corrupted souls could be challenging. A difficult choice. In particular, the bigger cities. Having to trust my gut. To seek the iron oracle of resolute instinct. In my experience, the only reliable method of finalising any such decision.

The desire to rid the World of these reprobates could grow into an irresistible mania. Planning and scheming became impossible, as a furious impatience to kill consumed my psyche. Whenever this occurred, travel became the balm for this itch. Flying to a warmer climate. Relaxing, seeking pleasure and hedonism. Becoming grounded. Intoxicating myself in the flesh-pits of tourism, or gambling. Boozing and living by a beach for a month would empty my mind of savage desires. For a while. Removing me from my private work, my secret life. Afterwards, the decision of which particular odious individual to make my next Target became much simpler. Based on the practicalities of a successful Hit. Rather than an emotional response to their character or crime.

ON THE LINE

One year, an early attempt at business investment compelled me to remain in London. From library archives, eight potential targets glared out. Each overdue for disposal. Nonetheless long months overseeing investment arrangements, dealing with a number of legal and contractual issues, cramped me. Leaving no room for studying any Target. The itch developed. A pining impossible to sate in decent company. Perhaps I'd studied those archives too long. Greater London seemed to attract or produce a stream of heartless characters who caused suffering to innocent people. Unable to decide who to kill. Or when the opportunity to kill them might arise. Knowing a hasty decision could lead me to making a mistake in the execution, travel once again seemed a good way to clear my mind. Once my commitments were no longer so intense, arrangements were made to go.

However, on this occasion my needs were more primal, less cordial. The usual distractions of casual tourism could not accommodate my urges. Flying out to Africa during the height of Beatlemania, after contacting some friends there from my time in the military, in search of conflict. Young men my age were strutting about London like prize peacocks. Meanwhile I became a mercenary. A junior officer in command of a company of hired killers. Raw men with nothing to lose and nothing to compare to the excitement of battle. Dogs of War. We all sought action. Real action. We found it. In one of Africa's most unstable, post-colonial countries. A place of raw natural beauty and humanitarian catastrophe. Systemically, a Third World hell-hole, damned by corruption. Sinking fast into the gaping abyss of civil war.

Into the fray with my life expose to severe risk. If deserving to die, if God wished me dead, then this adventure would provide ample opportunity. Yet despite the bullets, grenade fragments and mortar blasts which killed some of those under my direct command, and many others around me, I'd survived.

Wounded, at times. Recuperating, for a while. Scarred, for eternity. Within and without. Hardened. Forged in fire. Quenched in tears. Again, and again. We revelled in it. We ran together, in lethal packs, seeking, destroying. Incurring the wrath of tribal warlords. Whose warriors charged us through clouds of choking dust in old jeeps, lorries and even tractors, armed to the teeth with Soviet infantry weaponry. Death came too close for comfort, like a bad habit, on many occasions. Long, endless days of cat-and-mouse combat. Against an unpredictable enemy. After three months, only eighteen of us remained of the original sixty-two Westerners who'd joined the brigade at its inception.

The money we'd made for our dirty work seemed irrelevant. Although it helped, of course. Flying on a Catalina back to Johannesburg, nursing many bruises and several deep cuts and scrapes, my thoughts turned to those left behind. Those men were not going home. No graves marked their existence. Some of them had died right beside me. In those noteworthy moments, as the thrumming aircraft whirled above the fraught countryside to gain height, a feeling of divine blessing enveloped me. Never before as an adult having felt safer. London cobbles would be beneath my feet within a day. Doubt fell away faster than the tormented African landscape dropped from view. A smile spread across my face, leaning back in the chair, placing lace-fingered hands behind my head in triumphal inner peace and self-knowledge. I truly had been chosen and crafted to be an instrument of God's Wrath upon this Earth.

Sam Daniels.
Tel Aviv.
August 1993

PART ONE

THE SLOB

" **G**ood morning Mr Nettles."
"Is it?"

"Oh yes, it's another lovely warm day out there again today."

"Well why don't you sod off outside to enjoy the sunshine and stop annoying me then? If I needed your opinion on the weather, I'd ask you for it. Meanwhile what I do want is more coffee, and this time I'd like it to be hot."

"I do beg your pardon sir, sorry to have disturbed you." Her voice held neither sarcasm nor malice. Although the young waitress did look stunned. She turned and went through to the kitchen. I sat across the dining area of the hotel in a secluded alcove. The Target always parked himself in the same place. My current seat providing a surreptitious angle to scrutinise him from.

This Hit prompted the initial questions. Private, inner questions. About motives for murder. The idyllic location of the hotel belying the ferocious scheming and homicidal intentions of my true purposes for being there. In deepest Staffordshire. The kill itself took no time. One of my cleanest.

The Slob. Adam Justin Nettles. Had a personalised number plate, rare in those days. Loved the sound of his own voice. Which only ever complained, bullied or most often, boasted. Never gave praise nor thanks with earnestness or goodwill. Nothing but leering smiles and sneering arrogance, from a physical wreck of a man. Objectionable in appearance as well as manners. Bloated in body, pock-marked in face, stinking with flatulence. A personification of insincerity.

In error, I spent too much time in close proximity to The Slob's dishonourable presence. Listening to him talk to good, honest people just as he had to the waitress. The man displayed bad manners and disrespect at every opportunity. Causing hatred to grow in my bosom. An utmost, intense and tangible odium. Branding his name onto the darkest facet of my heart. Yet, such fervent sentiments cloud judgement. It would be nice to be able to tell you my hits were those of a professional. Emotionless. Sterile. Efficient. However, it would be a lie. I relished killing this horrible reprobate. Only the thought of one day being able to end his life with my own hands furnished me with enough perseverance to commit to the task. To do all the things necessary to getting the job done. To deny myself the comforts and pleasures of life, in order to learn his habits. All these sacrifices for one purpose. Strike The Slob from existence with cold efficacy.

⟫•◆•⟪

Business investments had bought me to Uttoxeter in The Midlands. A property venture. Which meant being in the area and visiting the sites proposed for the developments my money would be invested in. Only expecting to be in the town for a week, on the fourth day my lawyers advised me to remain in the vicinity a while longer. Minor complications over boundaries with the local authority and contractual negotiations compelled me to remain in the town. Soon though, the choice became one of lingering there in order to kill again. For during that first month, the Target had entered my awareness and drew my attention with magnetic compulsion.

A PERFECT DOZEN

W ealth facilitated my ability to invest. This came from items in my possession on return from Africa, in February 1967. Having been my third trip out to the continent. Naming the countries involved, is irrelevant here. Suffice to make note that these excursions incorporated several independent states of Western, Central and Southern Africa. Those who hired my services paid well, but that is not how my real fortune originated. As well as a suitcase crammed with various forms of African cash, eleven rare items also came to England upon my return. Their journey possible due to a curious combination and sequence of luck, sheer chance and blood-debt. Objects of immense value. Luxury items. Only for particular buyers, or collectors of such things. Apiece, they were unique and markedly different from one another. Huge worth being one factor they all had in common. Another being the fact they were all small enough to fly home with me. Perhaps when compelled to write another book, I shall tell the whole story of what these objects were and how each came to be mine. For now, a brief list shall have to suffice the curious.

A weapon. A relic. An egg. A nugget. A rock. A pelt. A gem. An amulet. An ingot. A bangle, and a heavy gold chain reputed to have come from a pirate, washed up dead upon the Angolan coast generations prior. Eleven unique artefacts which facilitated my entrepreneurial life.

OVERLY ENCOMPASSED

Studying The Slob tested my patience. Proximity to him bred contempt in me with resolute haste. Revolting, disrespectful and lacking social graces, he made it easy for anyone decent to despise him. Reeking of stale cigarette smoke, body odour and foul anal fumes, the odious beast revelled in his flatulence, arrogant and uncaring of others reactions.

His manner with service staff revealed the spite hidden beneath the practiced, disarming smiles. Manipulative, dismissive and malevolent, nothing else. The diametric opposite of the jolly fat-man characters who seem so much happier with themselves and bring joy to all around them. The more I studied The Slob, the more the prospect of murdering him excited me.

At one social function, The Slob displayed himself in all his glory; -

"Oh yeah, I told him to fetch me a file from the bottom drawer of my filing cabinet", he said in his thick Black Country drawl, "then I stood over him as he knelt there and let out a ripper of a fart, right on the back of his head! Nearly blew his bloody wig off! It stank too! I almost shat myself laughing!"

He guffawed, slapping the nearest bloke on the shoulder. The awkwardness tangible almost to the point of taste. His listeners laughter grew weaker as they pictured the plight of the poor clerk unfortunate enough to be employed by this abrasive individual. They stood stiff with embarrassment as he plied them with what he considered to be a humorous anecdote. At least one of the unfortunate half-dozen folk caught up in The Slob's pantomime thought he'd been lucky; - The chap's expression of disgust flashed rage. Signifying if *he* had been the fat man's intern, job or no job, he'd have reacted with violence to such calculated personal effrontery.

———◇———

Nearness to the malodorous Target started to cloud my thinking. Weeks of surveillance in boring circumstances grated my nerves. The man disgusted me. Overbearing, selfish and filthy. Getting to know his habits so well had me grinding my teeth whilst asleep. Sat uncomfortable in a hot car, waiting for him as he stuffed his face, nurtured the hate festering in my breast. The Hit became a matter of personal vengeance.

For a large built man, The Slob had a weedy, whiney voice. He attended so many social functions the opportunities to study him came with dependable regularity. The sound of his voice drilled into my brain. Even when observing him from afar, I knew those around him would be suffering his flatulence. No-one of good taste and manners could miss the deliberate and deplorable ignorance of the man. His ability to blunder through the awkwardness he created around himself astonished me. However, here lay the problem with getting to know the Target too well.

Something in me made it personal. In retrospect, the ineptness of my surveillance techniques being the main cause. Far too much time spent paying far too much attention. The Slob never knew I existed until the moment he died. Despite having been in the same room, attending the same function as him on numerous occasions.

———◇———

Sensing my judgement becoming impaired, I decided to back off. For over three months. Emotional attachment to killing this man clouded my focus, a break would help. Fortune lent a hand as business matters demanded my presence elsewhere. A new investment in a growing prestige car showroom in Loughborough required my full attention for a while to ensure its success. The call came just at the right time. After making the arrangements, I made the brief move over to Leicestershire.

⟫⟨◆⟩⟪

"Do you need an extra towel Mr Daniels?" The assistant asked on my way into the changing rooms. Glaring whiteness from his tennis-style health club clothing caused me to squint.

"No thanks but let me know after forty minutes if I'm not already out please", I asked.

"Of course."

"I have an appointment at half-two, wouldn't want to miss it."

"No problem, I'll see to it myself sir", he assured me with a winning smile. Nodded thanks back at him, then turned towards the door. Steam billowed around my feet as it swung open. A small sauna room on the opposite wall exuded heat and moisture. Swimming long hours at the country club exhausted the body, helping clarify thoughts. This went on week after week. When anger and impatience no longer drove intention, I allowed myself to begin thinking about ending The Slob's sorry existence once again. Until the time my presence became unnecessary in Loughborough, allowing my return to Staffordshire.

The Slob lacked the imagination to enjoy any spontaneous element to his weekly routine. Making tracking him easy. As long as he filled his gut, ate in one of his favourite restaurants and grasped every opportunity to be rude and ungracious to those serving him, the despicable ne'er-do-well felt happy with life.

GASBAG GARROTTED

One gloomy, cold evening in late November 1971 found me waiting. Beneath the cover of a large Eucalyptus in a shaded corner of The Slob's favourite restaurant's car park. A place South of the town centre, on the Cannock Road. The rear car-park backed onto a small riverbank. The sounds of water calmed me whilst standing dripping wet, enjoying the smell of freshly-wetted earth, close to his car. For several damp hours. My Barbour jacket kept me dry but the tips of leafless branches scratched across its waxed surface with undue volume. Drips formed rivulets down my nose. Cobwebs strung between the shrubs, clung to my eyebrows. Shuffling from foot to foot with discomfort, collar up against the rain, affected my patience before he finished stuffing his face. Despite all my efforts, these factors did get my blood up.

At last, The Slob came into sight. Coughing, dragging on a stubby cigar. Worries of the Hit being detected or disturbed evaporated. He'd indulged far too much to put up a fight or make any noise. Watching his last walk brought a smirk to my lips. Taking an age to shuffle and belch his way across the sloping asphalt expanse, had me clenching my jaw with a curious mixture of scorn and mirth. The door of his white 1968 Rover 2000 clicked open with little sound. He huffed and sweated his stinking carcass into the plush, squeaking leather seat. Knowing he'd leave his driver's door open to light a fresh cigar, puffing away as he always did for a minute or two prior to driving off, my heart pounded with anticipation and the sheer devilment of it.

The moment arrived. Stepping around the vehicle without a sound, my arm wrapped around his fat, lolling head, garrotting him. Two smooth, stubby pieces of polished Ash connected by eighteen inches of heavy-duty fence-wire made an effective tool. Robust enough for me to put all my strength and weight into pulling the wire tight across his bulbous throat. Abrupt, rushing anger raged through veins protruding out from wrists and hands, as they did their work with full exertion. Pent-up disdain fuelled latent savagery with explosive effect. Brawny arms, dreamlike and dis-connected, grabbed and gripped, knuckles whitened as grasping pressure hardened with hate. Twisting the contorting, reddening face around into my own, laughing at his complete lack of comprehension. The Slob died wondering who the hell I was.

"No-one likes you", I hissed into his gawking, bulging eyeballs as he lost the will and began to sag, life leaving him.

"You're a disgrace to the human race Adam. Die like the dog you are." The cigar burnt my hand in his pitiful, desperate, diminishing panic. A terror which also produced a vile billowing of hot piss and reeking, flatulence-propelled excreta, amid his shabby, flailing demise. Blood and mucus of some sort got onto my jacket whilst stuffing Adam back into his Rover. His filth hung on me as I trudged away into the dreary, callous night. Heavy rain on the two mile walk back to the car washed all traces of the foul deed off. Relief from the suppressed, pressurised mania of neglected bloodlust grew into euphoria and an invigorating rush of masculine power. The stinking fat bastard died like the sorry disgrace he'd been in life. Perfect.

<hr />

The corpse remained undisturbed until the next Monday morning, thirty-six hours later. The stink in there must have been remarkable. As in life, so in death. His car keys and the clothes I'd worn went into a street-bin, twenty miles away. All wrapped in sheets of newspaper stained with black shoe polish.

Savoured a fine Cuban cigar within an hour of ending Adam's sorry excuse for a life. Drank a glass of vintage port and listened to the Shipping Forecast on Radio Four. Overall, the job had felt great. From this point on my self-denial in taking pleasure from the grim work I'd chosen to undertake ceased. Knowing I couldn't stop it. Or wouldn't.

BLIND IGNORANCE

Did The Slob deserve to die in such an ignominious manner? He killed a dog whilst drunk-driving. A guide dog. The blind man holding the guide dog suffered non-fatal injuries, but hearing his dog's dying howls of pain and terror finished him off within minutes. Heart failure. Due to extreme stress and shock. The man and his dog were stood on a traffic island at the time. As were three young nurses. Two of whom Adam crippled, the other one suffered facial burns and became sterile due to her injuries.

She took an overdose eighteen months later. Her mother found her, she had her stomach pumped and survived. Next time the depressed former nurse with her life wrecked by the spiteful, conceited gas-bag made certain by hanging herself with her own stocking from a bridge over the River Trent at nearby Willingham. Indiscipline, booze and arrogance destroyed those lives. Money and influence whitewashed the guilty. God sent me to collect the debt.

Adam's money and influence bought a "loophole" lawyer, who saved him from prison. Not only prison. He kept his driving licence and even applied for compensation from the local authority for not having enough street lighting in the area the incident occurred. Never once showed remorse or any kind of thoughtful emotion towards the families, who all suffered from guilt and anxiety. The Slob drove like a maniac around the quaint streets of Uttoxeter, without a care for anyone in his way. My instincts told me he had yet more blood on his hands. Another dog walker. A cyclist, someone. Maybe my need to kill pushed these opinions. I believe both instinct and righteous fury honed me to the truth.

Killing The Slob had taken too long. Not to embroil myself seemed an obvious evolution. Not to seek personal justification for the choice of Target. Reminding myself these people were all reprehensible, shameful, contemptible individuals. I would have to keep my emotions impersonal and professional. Despite this Hit providing satisfaction, impatience to move location and select the next Target came within days of garrotting Adam. Fresh urges soon built within me. Somebody had to die by my hands. Just a matter of finding the right person who deserved it.

THE SCRUFF

The stony old city of Durham. Something drew me to the place. Large enough to offer plenty of potential Targets. Whilst staying there at The Grand Hotel a story kept being reported on local Wearside radio and tv news. Filtering into my consciousness over the course of several weeks. An interesting hearing at York Crown Court. Developments kept the attention of local media for over a month. The man at the centre of the case turned up a couple of years later. By pure chance. Or Divine Intervention. Whilst I was engaged in my Secret Service in another city, with another Target under surveillance. You will meet both these men later.

A bigger man's mutt. That's all The Scruff could ever have amounted to. The classic weaselly type. Slim, though not at all healthy. This weakling had narcissism nailed. A real-life Romeo. We've all met his sort. Greasy, dirty. A scruff. Always on the blag, scrounging. Tapping others for money and favours at all opportunities.

Threadbare. Down at heel. Sourcing most of his wealth from the unfortunate women who accommodated him. When the sly bastard did have to earn his keep, the cash wouldn't remain in his pockets very long. Blowing most of his wages at the nearest Bookmakers shop as soon as he could, whilst using girlfriend's money to fund his vices. My own experience with women indicated he must have something they liked. Lord knows, some of those who appeared to enjoy his company were attractive. Frequenting The Scruff's favourite haunts proved useful for getting to know his routines. Sitting way across the establishment, often with an escort, pondering on what his appeal could be.

"What does a woman find nice about a poorly turned-out bloke like him?" Shirley, my raven-haired, professional date for the night, chewed her gum and took a sip of her Babycham;

"Don't know. He does have nice eyes and good cheekbones though." On our third encounter in as many weeks, I felt comfortable pointing out my intended Target to "Shirley", though not in a way to indicate any of my savage intentions. Curiosity demanded it. Besides, By the time we parted ways the next afternoon, her memory had once again been filled with hours of energetic, satisfactory sex.

"But he's a wretch! Look at his shoes! Scruffy sod."

"Maybe he's well-endowed then", she offered with a cheeky grin.

"Must be, can't be much else!" We laughed and she cuddled into me, handing me my glass of gin.

"What about those three over there?" Pointing to a blonde lady stood between two gentlemen, taking her attention away from the guttersnipe I aimed to kill. We chatted a little more, then sat nodding to the music together, smiling and drinking, anticipating our business-like bonding of flesh, soon to follow.

The Scruff's features caught the shimmering disco lights. His pointy visage preceded the weedy, nasal voice, rising in tone with each word, regaling his latest woman with some farcical tale. Her shrill laughter, lonely as a desperate echo, followed the runt's miserable monologue.

What did they see in him? A drunk's charm perhaps? Unwashed hair, dishevelled clothes and missing teeth were the only things apparent to me. Although he did have a penchant for fast cars. The Scruff possessed a Vauxhall Firenza HP, one of only a few hundred ever produced. How he came to own it, remains a mystery to me unto this day. He tore around everywhere he went as if on a racetrack.

How did I choose to dispose of him? Well, live by the sword, die by the sword. For The Scruff, I took on the challenge of making the murder appear to be an accident.

———◇———

Nothing significant encumbered my efforts. To ensure he became trapped in his burning car on a lonely stretch of road. Torched alive in a cold, stone-walled ditch. The Scruff may have been dishevelled, but he did have regular habits. Such as where, when and how he drove to see a particular acquaintance. Country roads, a long open straight, a fast curve, a well-placed Foden seven and a half-ton pick-up truck, and cruel intent, all combined to ensure The Scruff met his searing fate at my hands.

I stepped down from the truck. Noticing he'd begun to recover from a knock to his head. The Firenza impacted the walls of the ditch at the side of the road hard, tyres screeching as they lay black stripes onto the cold tarmac. Smashing the driver's window with a crowbar, then pouring ethanol into his spluttering mouth and laughing as the deadly chemical splashed over him felt good. The Scruff screamed and thrashed in the rampant flames ignited by the Zippo lighter I tossed into the Vauxhall. Scorching fire burned into him for eternal seconds prior to the explosion of the fuel in the tank. Revving the truck up and away into the night, The Scruff's dying screams ringing in my ears, a prodigious sense of accomplishment glowing in my heart.

———◇———

Charles Adrian Hudsley. Thirty-nine years old. The Scruff. Learnt a lot about him through a barman named Sid at a pub called The Blue Boar. He and I grew familiar over the course of a few weeks. Spending cash in abundance each night caught his attention. Very easy for learning the gossip on the grapevine, bar staff. Bored to madness by the regulars. A businessman on a long stay, at the bar every night for a month or two, becomes a goldmine of fresh material to a bloke like Sid. Providing fresh talking points to bat back at the constant, slobbering drunks he had to deal with year in, year out.

Sid's knowledge proved useful. His specialist subject, Durham. A rum old city, full of intrigues, according to Sid. He claimed to know all the most notorious criminals, at least by name and reputation. He enlightened me a great deal about The Scruff as I'd pretended to be interested in buying one of the flats in the block he'd lived in. Where he left others to die.

I'd set myself up in Sid's pub, one of several The Scruff frequented. Sid's, a large corner-house establishment with enough room to remain anonymous, being best for my purposes. Dressing down a little, I'd sit at the quiet end of the bar wearing a cap and reading the racing papers on midweek afternoons. During the slowest days, a rapport between Sid and myself built up. After six weeks, he and I exchanged chat or gossip of all kinds whenever he came close to me.

"Nasty, cowardly piece of work he is", Sid gestured with his head, hands busy emptying ashtrays into a metal bucket.

"Who, the skinny bloke?" I asked. Curious Sid had chosen to speak about him. Had he noticed me stalking The Scruff?

"Yeah, the spineless turd left two old ladies to die in a fire. Made sure he got out himself, but folk reckon he'd caused it in the first place." He spat the words, not bothering to disguise his distaste.

"What? The fire? He lit it on purpose?" Keeping my voice full of earnest inquiry in an attempt to seem ignorant of all knowledge of the tragic deaths.

"No, not like that. But he was bloody careless. Those two old girls had no chance. The fire was an accident, but it was his fault it started and he made no attempt to help them get out." Sid explained in his tinny Wearside accent.

"Jesus Christ. That's cold-hearted." Conviction filled my words with sincerity. It seemed Sid really did have a personal dislike for The Scruff and revelled in telling anyone he could about him. But then, he did have to serve the horrible rotter on a regular basis. Familiarity to these types does indeed breed a fierce contempt for them.

"You said it. I don't like him drinking in here to be honest but there's nothing I can do, unless he does something stupid enough to get himself barred. He's a wheedling, lying bastard. Those old girls were good neighbours to him. My ex-wife's mam knew one of them. Those two lived below his place, in that small block of flats. He knew them, they helped him out plenty of times. Usually when he had no money for food due to losing it all down the bookies. But he never bothered helping them when it really mattered. He knew he was leaving them to die as far as I'm concerned. I can't fucking stand the bloke."

These particular words of Sid's, the last spoken through gritted teeth, were more than sufficient. From that moment, The Scruff became the subject of yet more intense focus. Through Sid's inside gossip, details from press reports and a later inquest, the story unveiled itself.

———————⊰•◆•⊱———————

The address proved difficult to pinpoint. Due to the topography of the estate and the numerous similar, three-storey flat-blocks in the vicinity. With a maze of footpaths and passageways woven betwixt them. These pathways wended between hedgerows, grass banks and the buildings. Joining a variety of small residential car-parks placed at intervals on the hillside, each connected to the single access road weaving through the estate.

A drab place of hidden horror. Upon discovery in pissing rain on a sun-less day, unnerving, ghostly. The thought of how the two elderly ladies died in there disturbed me. Knowing the block as soon as it came into view. Evidence glared with subtle eeriness. Their block had been re-fitted. Whitewashed and re-designed. With new facias, doors and windows. Yet nothing could ever wash away the dread atmosphere emanating from the place.

———————⊰•◆•⊱———————

Charles had abandoned his vulnerable neighbours when they needed him most. Both succumbed to the smoke and flames. The fire started because of him. The ladies were neighbours, occupying the lower-most residencies, two for each floor of the building. Their floor being half-below true ground level. Set into a steep hillside, with landscaping to allow for windows. The pathways and stairwells around their two properties had been well-kept all year round. The scruffy toe-rag tapped those two ladies for everything he could get. If he did manage to do anything useful for them, perhaps mowing a lawn, collecting or delivering large items or shopping, he took much more payment than he'd earned. Then having the cheek to pocket small change from their purses behind their backs as he sat and sipped their coffee, before bragging about doing so to his cronies later, in the pub. He'd been disliked and distrusted by many for his attitude towards his elderly neighbours long before the tragedy.

The Scruff had lived above them. Allowing his landing to become full of detritus, litter and leaves. Maples, Oaks, and Hornbeams clustered the hillside, surrounding the flat-block from above. Years of leaf-fall had built up around the last few yards of the landing. Of course, in Charles' mind, no-one needed to walk beyond his front door. He deemed the task of clearing the area unnecessary.

'An indolent waster. Idle, lacking empathy and shame.'
'A four-star low-life alright. Scum of the Earth.'
'He shall hardly even be missed. This work has to be done.'
'It will be my pleasure.'

The Scruff had discarded a cigarette. Whilst struggling with keys and drunkenness, fumbling to open the door. Hot weather, neglect, and a vortex formed between the building and the steep landscape, all combined to create a flaming whorl of evil luck. The cigarette butt smouldered in amongst the bone-dry leaves. Fire broke out. The bins to the property were stored below the end of the block. Around the corner and below the initial flames licking onto Charles' window frames. Burning leaves, litter and embers blew down into the refuse, setting alight old newspapers and rags.

A fearsome conflagration ensued. Blasted by wind and fuelled by plastics, wood and lead paint, it swept around the lowest floor of the block. Devilish tongues of searing flame scorched into open windows, alighting net curtains and polystyrene ceiling tiles within minutes. Both women died awake, one trapped in her hallway, the other lasted a little longer in her bathroom. The drunken mutt slept through most of it. Only waking up as sirens grew close. He ran from his door and never looked back. The damage left clues to the cause of the fire, yet not enough evidence existed to effect an arrest or trial. The enquiry remained only at the coroner's level. The Scruff owed those ladies many favours, Sid had told me. I felt he owed them his life. Through me they got it.

THE POSEUR

Short, swarthy, thick-set, with long hair receding and thinning on top. Revealing too much forehead. Much to The Poseur's chagrin. Beard straggling into chest hair. Self-absorbed. Image conscious yet lacking natural beauty. Laughable. Lots of time spent looking in the mirror. A good proportion lifting weights. Plenty more chasing impressionable young women. Much younger, half his own age.

Not that I cared. A man must do what a man must do. The temptations of an eager young lover are enough to break anyone's resolve. Although this is not the case here. The women were neither eager or interested, but The Poseur's money talked. Weeks of surveillance provided abundant evidence for accurate characterisation of the man.

Vainglorious in words. Pusillanimous in deeds. A liar, a fake, a show-off. Always assuming he looked magnificent. In reality, looking foolish. Arms, chest and shoulders over-developed. Back and torso much less so, with no backside and scrawny legs. It seemed his mirror did not reach below his ribcage.

Archibald 'Archie" Cunliffe. Owner of a handful of small businesses. A private, members-only gymnasium, a laundrette, a corner-shop and an old mill he had converted into a set of private apartments. Between these he earned enough to own a classy MGB GT Coupe and keep himself dressed in the latest fashions. He listened to rock bands, buying the latest L.P. records and playing them on an expensive home stereo. Using imagery to look younger and fashionable. Cut-off denim jacket, torn jeans and black boots.

A confused individual. Too straight to be a biker, yet too vain to dress straight. Punching above his weight and using every trick in the book to do so. He lived in Weston-Super-Mare. A place I never stayed at. Preferring instead to hotel in Bath and Bristol, alternating monthly. My latest investments were centred around a company based in Newport, Gwent. Knowing my accent would make me stand out in Cardiff or Swansea, I chose to remain on the English side of the Severn. However, my accent came to be a talking point there anyway.

⟫◆⟪

"Up from London?", the brown-eyed waitress spoke with an attractive West-Country drawl. "Trains delayed again I heard", despite her attempts to sound less so. She began pouring my pot of tea.

"Yes, I heard. Been here a few days already though. So, I wasn't affected." She handed me the steaming cup. "Thank you." The Victoria hotel in Bristol had been my home for three days at that point. The Bone China cup and saucer made an alarming amount of noise for such a quiet restaurant.

Settling into the Chippendale furniture in my Tweed threads felt as good as anywhere. Although despite attempts at creating an atmosphere of opulence, the Victoria failed. Nothing to complain about. Simple things. Obvious restructuring jobs. Rooms created by dividing one large suite, with asymmetrical results. Leaving a wanting. A need to have seen the original structure in all its glory.

"Well, I took the start of the week off", the waitress's gentle tone and delayed response breaking my train of thought.

"Oh, were you ill?"

"No, it's my shift rotation. We work seven days on, then get three days off."

"Do you like it like that?"

"You get used to it. Shame though, otherwise I'd have met you sooner. Most of our guests are a bit stuffy. You're nice though."

"Thanks, but I'm still glad to have missed those traffic jams."

"Makes sense. I would too. Like I said, you're lucky. Some folks were stuck for hours. On trains, in the station. It's absurd. To be sat wanting to travel, stuck on a stuffy train, or windy platform, surrounded by all the other poor sods. And everyone fed-up. You were lucky all right." The dusky waitress's voice had a lovely soft lilt to it.

"I certainly was." Wishing her to be silent my mind had work to do, but somehow, she aroused me. Instinct told me the waitress felt the same way. Running my eyes along her curves, whilst turning in the seat to face her, our eyes met. Lustful thoughts laid bare for each other to see. The quality of her perfume cut through the aroma of smoke and food, announcing itself with pleasant, sweet fragrances. My spontaneous smile upon getting a good whiff of it surprised me.

"You're not from London yourself though?" She asked, taking the lead.

"That's right, I come from Middlesex. How can you tell?"

"From the way you speak. Sort of old fashioned. It's nice." She began twirling a strand of hair between the fingers of her left hand.

"I speak old fashioned?"

"Sort of, well, you're polite and well-spoken. You don't sound like the regular London types we get in here", she asserted without raising her voice or becoming defensive. Her candour impressed me and I couldn't help but warm to her.

"No, don't suppose I do", I replied, smiling and holding her gaze. "You have a lovely voice yourself sweetheart." My brazen, seductive eyes set her on fire. She had to look away, finding an uncleared table nearby a convenient distraction. Feeling her response brewing as she settled herself, I pushed my back into the seat to create space. A pause lingered between us. She slowed her motion down, Considering her words.

"You gonna tell me then?", her voice piped after a couple of minutes. Not understanding her meaning, I raised an eyebrow. "Would you like to order some food in your crafty London accent, Mr Blue Eyes?" She knew what to say.

"Middlesex is within Greater London," I winked. Certain she would neither know nor care if my words held any geographical truth.

"Middle-sex, eh? Is that what they're calling it now? Take's all sorts I suppose", she replied with a wink of her own. I laughed, a mere chuckle, but it still seemed loud in the staid atmosphere of the hotel restaurant. My table occupied a kind of booth, sheltered from the rest of the diners for privacy but with an outstanding view of the Severn and the Brecon Beacons beyond. Feeling a moment of intimacy between us, I decided to enlighten the pleasant woman. With a smile to disarm her, words flowed as my eyes held hers.

"My family travelled a lot during my youth, my accent took a while to become what it is today."

"Well, I like it. It's nice." Her smile melted my indifference and I noticed the allure of her shape again as she moved around the table.

"I suppose you get around a lot, then?", she looked straight at me with a penetrating gaze. Right then we both knew we would end up getting acquainted later that night. Our talk grew more and more lurid each time she served my table. After her shift ended, we met out in my red, 1972 Lotus Europa. We sped off out of town and through the hills racing up to Gloucester and back before daybreak.

We first had sex on the bonnet. Face to face, her legs locked around my hips. The heels of her stilettoes scratched my backside and the car's road springs squeaking put me off my rhythm. So, we had it up against the driver's door instead. She responded well to the rough but unhurried coupling. A knot became untwisted with the knowledge my exertions had sated both of us. Her hair slid through my fingers with silky smoothness as we caressed between copulation. After getting dressed we held each other in a warm embrace. Albeit as we parted, I remained cordial but aloof. "Okay, we're here, glad you've enjoyed yourself. It's been lovely spending time with you, so happy we met this morning. Seems so long ago already." I said whilst parking up to drop her off.

"Yeah, you've been really kind. Would be nice to spend time with you again", the waitress smiled, picking up her sleek purple handbag, "Any chance of it?"

"Of course. I'll be around for a few weeks."

"But no promises? You know I don't want romance. If you have no intention of doing so you don't have to pretend", her voice hardening a little with these assertions.

"I know. I'm not pretending. You take it easy. See you soon", I said, pulling her close for a parting kiss on the lips.

"Be good", she called as I began to reverse the Lotus.

"No promises, remember?" I laughed. We exchanged sincere, eloquent smiles.

'If only she knew.'

'If only she knew what?'

'If only she knew the real you.'

'Yeah, if only. Nobody knows the real me.'

'Nobody needs to.'

PAPER TIGER

"Don't allow yourself to weaken, be like me!" Cheap words springing out in bright orange from the garish advertising poster.

"I won't weaken until you're done, you can rely on that much", my voice growled back at the unimaginative marketing. Stood outside The Poseur's gymnasium on a dusty road in a grimy part of town. An unimposing, anonymous place, drab and uninspiring. It could only look better within.

The poster seemed incongruent to say the least. A picture of Archie lifting a dumbbell in one hand, pointing at the observer with the other. In the style of the iconic, Lord Kitchener First World War recruitment poster; -

"Your Country Needs You!" - Except in this case, Archie also had a slim, swimsuit-clad blonde with her arm around his waist alongside him.

The Poseur's vanity ensured he never associated with those who could show him up. The real body-builders and weightlifters would have failed to be impressed by his kind. His gymnasium being marketed towards a more middle-class, less aggressive clientele. Archie loved to promenade himself up and down his establishment in a vest and loose jogging pants. Impressing the young men who bought into his fakery and a few girls he employed as reception staff. However, he avoided training in front of others. Ultimately, he lacked confidence. Deep down, Archie knew he lacked good looks, a domineering physique or even an attractive persona. Due to these shortcomings, he had a mechanic's garage converted into his own private gym. In there he spent hours lifting barbells and posing in front of mirrors, enjoying the sounds of his favourite rock albums whilst huffing, puffing, and pumping iron.

———◆———

"I can get that if you like", the porter at the discreet yet modern motel just outside Bath offered, reaching for my suitcase.

"Thank you but there's no need", I replied, resistant to engaging him.

"Please, I insist. You look tired and besides, I need the exercise." He didn't but his enthusiasm melted my resolve.

"Ok you talked me into it." I said, smiling at his affable manner.

"Room forty-four, isn't it?", he asked.

"It is. Thank you. Very observant."

"Not rocket science, is it? Been here long enough to know what's going on from one day to another. Yours is the Lotus, isn't it? Can't miss the thing. I love that model. Love their Formula One team as well. Got to support the home teams. Especially when they're the underdogs."

"Absolutely. Can't argue with that", I answered. Then, "Yes, the Lotus is mine."

"Thought so. I like to imagine myself driving round the Italian Alps in a car like yours. You been very far in it?"

"This is the furthest from London she's been up to yet. Only had her a few months. Lovely motor for what it is, but not so practical. Not sure about the colour either. Originally, I wanted racing green, but there were none available at the time." Attempting to parry his bombardment of queries and observations with as much information as possible.

"Hmmm, yeah. You could always have a re-spray", the porter offered, seeming to agree with me about the colour. The whole conversation taking place as we made our way in the lift the short hop up two floors, then along the inevitable corridor of doors to my room.

"Here we go, forty-four. All yours."

"Thank you. Here, get yourself a drink or two." I said, handing him a crisp new fiver.

"I certainly will! Thanks very much indeed sir. Anything you need, let me know. I'm here most days 'till around eight in the evening."

"Good stuff, I'll bear that in mind, thank you." My response whilst opening the door. The happy porter turned away, walking tall. This exchange convinced me to buy a different car to use for this Hit. The Lotus would be good to be seen in. Then I'd become associated with it. For the Hit, any innocuous vehicle would do. Perfect. I thanked the porter again *in absentia* for this added detail to my murderous plans, feeling extra satisfaction for having just tipped him so well.

———◆———

Observing The Poseur from the roof-space instigated a bout of pure hate. Impersonal dis-like transmuted into spiteful detestation. His personal gym occupied a rear extension to large, Olde-Worlde building, which had a shop front on the busy street on the far side. Built of solid red brick, topped with a tiled roof comprised of Welsh slate. A sturdy steel drainpipe provided nimble access. Decades of dust and neglect gave the roof-space a strong musty odour. Though I knew about this from a practise run a few weeks prior and had come prepared. A dark blue silk scarf purchased in Cambridge in the Summer of '72 kept the worst of the dust out.

Archie's weakness magnified before me. Pushing himself but overworking his arms and chest. I couldn't understand why he hadn't included an exercise bike in his gymnasium. His legs looked comical. He became quite a sad character to me during those intimate moments of surreptitious surveillance. When he thought himself alone, without an audience. Feeble, lacking authentic confidence. All at once, pity stirred, rising in my heart.

'If you pity him now, how can you kill him?'
'Watch me.'
'Maniac.'
'You should know.'
'Perhaps. The question is, do you?'
'What do you think?'
'Only you know the answer to that.'

Crushing and grinding pity between clenched teeth kept my heart hard and intentions cruel. Allowing scorn to temper grim determination. Motivating murderous intentions with righteousness. These were to be The Poseur's last moments of life. Within the hour I'd be miles away, breathing cool fresh air. He'd be another corpse left in my wake.

GRIP

Possessing the power to choose the precise moment to end another's life. Such a glorious privilege. Becoming a fiendish game in the tight, discomforting confines of the dusty roof-space. Delight elbowing pity aside, as The Poseur's fatal surprise loomed ever closer. Discerning he preferred certain songs, roused interest. He got up to replay the same few tracks at the start of a particular cassette more than once. However, the circumstances of my position in the roof-space were deteriorating. Over-riding choices. Compelling extreme, ferocious action.

Sweat boiled from my head, forming rivulets. Rolling and dripping from my nose and eyelids. Breathing became difficult as the air became foul with my own exhaled breath. Knowing the scarf had to remain in place, I attempted to calm down. But the dreadful pounding music and cramped conditions drove me to madness. Plan A fast became redundant. Whilst wondering if any Plan B existed, events took on a life of their own.

Constricted breathing and dripping heat made me giddy. Unable to re-position without making a noise, I lay still. Time went by and my state worsened ever further. Minutes stretched. Awful songs tormented. Further inactivity became impossible. Thoughts spilled into overdrive. The drastic need to take action boiled over in me to produce an immediate and violent response to the unique set of circumstances.

Smashing down through the ceiling onto Archie hurt me, although less than it did him. Pain flashed through one thigh and both feet. Most of the impact went to his lower abdomen and groin. He saw me dropping onto him as he bench-pressed the loaded barbell. His eye's bulging out with exertion and shock.

"Wha? -Aaarrrgghhoothfftch!" A huge gasping groan blew out of him as my fall timed with his lift. The heavy steel weight dropped onto The Poseur's chest as he spluttered, screeching for air, hands trapped by his sides, head thrashing up, down and side to side. He kicked, struggling to sit up. Pulling myself off the floor and ceiling-tile debris, I scrambled up and grabbed the barbell before he could recover.

Hearing, "Now you're for it ya bastard!" Hissing through hard-gritted teeth surprised me. Followed by; "You're not strong at all, are you? You can't stop me killing you can you Archie? Bet you thought you were gonna live forever, well look at you! You don't look so good now!" The words disembodied. As if hissed by someone else. Some maniac full of violent energy. By this point pure hate and frightful rage had consumed my mind.

Fingers wrapped around knurled grips still warm and sweaty from Archie's efforts. Whilst holding the steel bar, sat astride him on the bench, ramming it down onto his throat, time slowed down. Frame by frame, filling me with strident power. Dread supremacy. Fleeting moments of bombastic passion, pulverised into perpetuity by their sheer solemnity. The fabric of time itself seemed palpable. A thumping pulse the only sound my ears perceived. The Poseur died in a frenzy of squawking, grunting and screeching, but none of it got through to me. Not at the time.

Archie's nostrils exploded mucus and blood into my face. Hands clawed, fingers scratched and clasped, desperate to push me off. His back bucked and feet kicked high, but a quick knee to the balls took the fight from him. Yet The Poseur did not die easy. Fists struck out, puke, blood and spittle kept spattering my face. Disgust and fury had me ramming the barbell up and down, time after time, onto his shattered windpipe. The weight of it became tiresome, compelling me to rub and roll it up under his chin instead, crunching and crushing all beneath. The sensation reminded me of my eldest sister, decades prior, showing me as a young boy how to crush biscuits with a rolling pin, in order to make a base for cheesecake.

Whether Archie asphyxiated or died of a heart attack is uncertain. But he did take too long to succumb for comfort. This crushing and constriction continued a minute or so, until at last, a massive spasmodic twitch flicked through his body, followed by complete stillness. He slumped, limbs out-stretched, resembling a starfish. My grip slackened and the barbell rolled off the warm corpse, falling to the wooden floor with a clattering thump.

The neat gymnasium had become a scene of barbaric horror. Blood dripped and congealed in puddles beneath the weight-lifting bench. Not my best work. Although The Poseur's music had covered the noise of the unnecessary struggle. Leaving the fresh corpse among the mess and wreckage and cleaning myself up, took only one song, as the awful music still clamoured out from the cassette player.

Up through the broken ceiling. Out across the back of the rooftop. A five-minute walk down dark, cobbled back-alleys and passageways to the innocuous car, a mustard-yellow Renault Scimitar. A nice little Shooting Brake. 'Perhaps not so innocuous,' I thought on approaching the bright and attractive motor, 'But still a step down from the Lotus.' After tuning the radio and allowing the engine to warm, a short drive took me to a quiet place to park up by the shore of the Bristol Channel. Moonlight and streetlights danced in shimmering reflections across the dark expanse of flittering water. A long sigh left cold lips as the engine juddered to a stop and I leaned back into the seat.

'*Time for a cigar, you've earned it.*'

'*Have I?*'

'*A job well done; don't you think?*'

'**My work here is done, yes. Whether I did it well, is not for me to say.**'

'*No, it's not. But you still know.*'

'**I still know what?**'

'*You know.*'

'**Behave.**'

'*You wish.*'

Time to reflect. An untidy Hit. Questions began nagging at my mind. Self-control, personal discipline and handling emotional reactions had always felt within my power. These moments of madness had to end. Accepting responsibility for the inability to employ restraint, would facilitate control of these inhuman desires. Or so I thought.

'What got into you?'

'Rage. Pure hate. Bestial instinct.'

'Correct.'

Why had this Target angered me so much? Had those last moments spent watching him really been so uncomfortable? Unbearable to the point of madness? Had familiarity alone bred such explosive contempt? Could any of these answers satisfy the nagging questions of morality? The Truth glared with an unblinking eye. My urgency to kill had become spontaneous, unrestrained rage. Could a variety of dissimilar influences have triggered such a messy conclusion to a well-planned job? Or had a single factor broken my self-control? Questions rattled through my brain. Each on its own track, waiting to be answered.

NECROTIC NEGLECT

The Poseur had neglected his duties as a landlord. A cheap conversion of the property and his indifference to the concerns of its tenants, led to the tragic deaths of three teenagers. Crushed beneath a steel fire-escape, which collapsed due to lack of upkeep. Two girls danced to pop music coming from a radio, provided by one of three lads taking turns having sex with their best friend on the level below. Causing the structure to lean out and pull the retaining bolts from the wall. But the bricks softened by a leaking gutter, dripping wet for years, were the ultimate cause.

Archie had ignored the problem. He could have prevented the teenagers from using his building to do as they pleased by installing a simple gate. An easy repair to the guttering in due time would have prevented the leak and kept the structure stable. Many times, one lady tenant in particular had reported the seepage. According to her it had leaked a torrent during heavy rain and created huge, dangerous icicles in sub-zero temperatures. The lady resident had been interviewed by a local tv news crew following the tragedy. Her angry words, recorded in the archives, had convinced me Archie should be the next Target; -

"He'd rather spend money on impressing younger women, on his vanity, than his duties as a landlord. He hasn't got a shred of decency in him. Never once concerned himself with the safety of us tenants. We're the ones who provide the cash to fund his lifestyle. He spent thousands of pounds on flying out to the Mediterranean just to get into bed with some young floozy. Never even thought about the condition round the back of this property", she'd said when interviewed.

'Kill him for her.'

'For who?'

'For the old lady. Must have been a great shock.'

'He will die for his own sins.'

'Are you sure he won't die for yours?'

The Poseur's place could have been much nicer. The building itself still retained much of its original beauty. Instead, it had become plain at best under his ownership. Two girls and one boy died beneath those steel steps. Two of the others were maimed. The Poseur evaded any criminal charges due to an expensive lawyer exploiting a technicality. Instinct, as well as rumour told me he'd paid to keep his freedom. Well, neither money nor social influence could help him now.

WOMEN, CRICKET & GOLF

A murderous lifestyle necessitated keeping women at arm's length. Remaining reserved but dutiful towards any women in my life balanced the opposing needs of intimacy and confidentiality. I found by treating my dates well, being aloof but always a gentleman, things tended to work out best. Setting and sticking to ground rules kept me free to pursue the real game. The only hunt that really mattered. The game of homicide.

After each Hit, breaking contact with any girlfriends in the area soon followed. By necessity. A few gifts, sent as way of an apology, helped ease my conscience. Once they'd figured I'd moved on, at least they'd remember being treated with respect. These factors were important, as some of those girlfriends had high hopes and perhaps even a genuine tenderness for me. My intention being to always leave them better off than I'd found them. Quite the opposite to the result of the violent interactions with me experienced by my Targets.

These were my own moral standards to live by, such as they stood. Methods of sating the instinctive, physical needs of adulthood. Apart from the obvious distractions of women, my other passions included travelling to all the classic grounds of England to watch quality cricket. Following the England team at home games, most of all whenever they were hosting The Ashes. An afternoon spent in the warm, open air at The Oval, Lord's, Trent Bridge, Old Trafford or Headingly afforded exquisite relaxation. County cricket sufficed if the international tests were not playing. At times this could benefit with meeting prospective business partners, or people seeking investment. I would mention the cricket and my desire to be at the test, then offer them lunch in the clubhouse to show me their proposal. Playing golf helped in this way too.

Not my favourite pastime, but the idyllic settings and a good walk, were motivation enough. My handicap remained respectful due to a great coach; whose services improved my game to a level suitable enough for the more exclusive private golf clubs. Membership of several of these notable clubs up and down the country became a necessity for business. Golf equalled commerce, not pleasure. These activities helped me detach from the urges of the darker parts of my mind. However, as you will discover in a later chapter, even playing golf opened an opportunity to kill another coward with innocent lives on his hands.

THE CROOK

From the West Country to East Anglia. Quite a contrast. For my murderous intentions though, business as usual. A slow train to Cambridge provided a relaxing means of travel. From there, out farther East into the Fenlands. In Norwich a Triumph dealership supplied a fresh car for a chunky wad of cash. A brand-new 1974 Mark IV Spitfire, designed by Giovani Michelotti, with the full-length wooden dashboard. Soft-top, British Racing Green. A little beauty. The sales manager's eyes opened wide, glistening with raw emotion as the money came to light. Clammy hands grasped mine, shaking it for the fourth time since I'd paid for the motor.

"Thank you, Mr Daniels, thank you!"

"No problem Dereck, you've been very helpful, I really appreciate it. The car's perfect. Just what I need."

"I'm glad to hear it. Has Josephine given you all our contact details?" Sales manager Dereck asked, keen to ensure my full gratification with the purchase and their service.

"She has, yes. All done", looking over towards Josephine their secretary, I flashed her a smile of appreciation.

"Give us a ring anytime you need to book a service or anything at all. And if you're in the area, drop in, we'll all be happy to help however we can." Dereck opened the door for me as he spoke and walked me to my new car.

"I'll do that Dereck, thank you."

The pleasant fellow couldn't smile wide enough. An agreeable opportunity for me to generate good feelings all round. To make someone's day, give the staff of the place an early finish on a Friday by purchasing the most expensive car in their showroom, with no expense spared. It helped me use some of the money accumulating in my accounts.

I rented offices in a large old building on a private square just off Bond Street in London. Mary, my ever-efficient "secretary" who organised all my business arrangements, would no doubt have told me to keep the receipt and claim the Triumph as a business expense, but exhausting my money solved more problems than it created. Acquisition of money had ceased to be a cause for concern years prior to my killing spree.

SELFISH SILVERFISH

Another region, another town. A new temporary home, this time a motel outside Bury St Edmonds. The libraries of Bury and Ipswich provided a Target after a few short weeks of searching. The low-life chosen on this occasion stood out for one reason. The Crook's selfish indifference caused multiple deaths, and affected many more people connected to the victims of his ambition. Most of them being their dependants. The Crook - a man from a small town which had no other claim to fame than being ugly, industrial and smelling of fish. Therefore, he had always lied, telling people he came from the far more fragrant and picturesque city of Norwich.

Phil Guy. Intelligent, self-assured, well-connected. In his own mind, untouchable. He knew nothing dirty would ever stick to him. He kept himself too clean. A prospective councillor, Phil had ambition. A civil servant of the mediocre kind. A senior manager of an uninspired section of the local authority's service.

However, The Crook only saw the opportunity to line his own pockets. Then, affect favours from those above him in the social spheres he aspired to be amongst. With access to vehicles and equipment, Phil kept a few key colleagues under him in his pocket. Booking a crew in for overtime each weekend. Having them use the equipment as sub-contractors, wearing different work clothes and do jobs for a company his brother owned. On hire to farmers or land-owners further inland. Clearance work in most instances.

Phil Guy disguised corrupt activities with smarm and charm. Convincing smiles and insincere handshakes. He loved a scam and used any leverage he could, however unethical, to support his own agenda. Unreasonable in all negotiations. A worthy Target. A sneering bully. Everything The Crook encouraged people to know about him, had been crafted. To play some part in his pantomime.

———◆———

The Crook loved to play overlord of his diminutive empire. Being corrupt failed to satisfy the entirety of his spite. The staff under him had a nothing but a rough time. He never gave an inch, nor any trust. Not even to those who deserved it. Being so avaricious and mean-spirited affected his perceptions. Judging everyone by his own standards. Phil lacked anything amounting to sincerity. Therefore, he couldn't recognise genuine commitment in others. For these reasons, people left good jobs to be free of his constant hectoring. Causing instability and upset among families and households he could otherwise have provided decades of stability for. All driven by political motivations. Surrounding himself with cronies. Using these tactics and outright Nepotism to strengthen his own position and influence. Aping his political peers, who went about their own business in much the same cut-throat manner.

———◆———

The Crook's misdeed came from a need to impress. Having to reduce spending and create income to meet financial goals set out by his dogmatic masters. Desperately wanting to elevate himself out of a mundane job and join these political ranks led him to make fatal decisions. Four men drowned for his vanity. Engulfed in a torrent of muddy, cold sea-water. A fifth man survived seven months before succumbing to respiratory problems, caused by the tragic, avoidable events of a fateful, yet otherwise ordinary evening.

———◆———

'This hit requires a cool head. Relaxed, emotionless.'
'As a hangman would be?'
'I suppose so. Why?'
'Does the hangman take pleasure from his work?'
'Why else would he do it?'

'You would enjoy it.'
'Yeah, probably.'
'Would you be tempted to taunt those about to swing with spite-filled whispers?'
'I doubt it.'
'But the stench of their fear would enrage you!'
'Behave. I would treat them with dignity and pull the lever.'
'Do you realise how deluded you truly are? That would never be enough for you.'
'Just stop.'
'True though, isn't it?'

Internal arguments can be difficult to ignore or resolve. But then, what *would* I do under those circumstances? Taunt the condemned before pulling the lever? Tie the knot in such a way so the neck didn't snap outright? In order to have them linger betwixt life and death, for brief, yet eternal moments of gasping, desperate agony?

Wondering didn't help. It only facilitated my mind to imagine evermore sadistic deeds. Planning became my focus. Meticulous planning. Keep one's mind occupied. Attempting to ignore the growing thrill at the thought of ending The Crook's despicable existence.

Establishing the location took a lot of surveillance. Phil had habits, but an irregular schedule. Working out the sequence of his activities facilitated predicting his whereabouts. This involved a heap of work. The Crook always remained unpredictable. Once I'd decided on the location, he gave me the slip time and again. On three occasions I'd waited in vain. At the place logic said he would show up, sooner or later. The fourth time Lady Luck shone down on my endeavours. Yet, in the end, it didn't matter. Fourth, fifth, seventh. In due course he would turn up whilst I awaited him there.

Phil had to attend regular meetings between local business leaders and councillors. Merely as an advisor. Always held on a mid-week morning. Afterwards, he'd travel alone in his car. I'd followed The Crook to the location several times. He'd walk by a stretch of canal, carrying a pair of binoculars. Bird-watching. Remaining there for several hours each time. The location being very secluded, yet really only a few miles from the urban world he inhabited. Nothing but the sound of the wind gusting and Gulls screeching. If any, only a handful of vehicles would ever be seen parked along the last mile or two of the lanes leading to the spot. Hikers, or more bird-watchers I presumed. Few and far between. Perhaps the occasional rogue fisherman, trying his luck out-of-season.

Only this locality in Phil's life had everything for a suitable manner of murder. Compelling me to adapt and become creative. I purchased a Land Rover and a small Kayak. Hiding the boat in a thick belt of reeds close to the spot early one morning, within easy access for when needed.

WILD FOUL

O n the day, we were alone. The whole area deserted of cars. After ensuring he intended to remain a while, I decided The Crook's time to die had arrived. Parking further up the road with access to the canal, walking to the reeds and unhitching the Kayak, took a good half-hour. Enough time for him to walk a mile along the lonely waterway. Another twenty minutes for me to paddle up to where he stood, gazing across the landscape. An open, placid mere rested across a narrow field on the western side of the canal. Wading birds and waterfowl created a humming cacophony of hoots and calls around the water's edges. The Crook's attention remained focused upon a cluster of noisy birds on the far side of the lake.

A cool breeze made progress in the Kayak slow. The exposed skin of my face glowed with cold. I had gloves and a partial wet-suit, as well as a wind-resistant jacket but the low temperature caught me out. Realising my body would become too stiff to be competent enough for the murder before very long, compelled an increase to the rate of paddling. The effort dragging on cold, wet shoulders.

Pulling up on the canal-side surprised Phil. He having attempted to ignore the approaching sounds of paddling and heavy breathing up to that point, by maintaining a steadfast gaze across the Mere opposite. Making plenty of noise to indicate being out of breath, I pulled the boat against the large edging stones with a scraping thump. An iron ring for fastening boats helped me stabilise. Then sat waiting to catch his eye. As much as he wanted to be alone, or wanted to ignore me, he couldn't. But the last thing he expected from me is what happened.

"Good afternoon, sorry to interrupt you." Not wanting to alarm or irritate, I spoke in my best voice in order to disarm him. I needed him to come close, within reach. "Excuse me, bit out of breath." He turned, allowed his binoculars to rest on his chest by their neck-strap and smiled.

"Oh, no problem. Can I help?"

"Have you seen another like me? My friend. In another canoe. He is moving much faster; my leg is hurt."

"No, I've not come across anyone else. Not been here very long myself though." He looked more exasperated than irritable. His desire for me to leave him thickened the silence. Using one oar to steady myself, I kept his attention a few seconds longer.

"He does move fast, too fast for me. I can't keep up with him, my leg is cramped. Not to worry though, he'll turn around and come back for me. Any chance you could help me disembark? Sorry to be a pain, the cramp is torturing me. My legs are locked, I can't push myself out properly. Do you mind? Just a quick pull should do it. I'll slide out this thing and onto the edge." He stared at me for a few seconds. I swear he rolled his eyes mentally. But his fear of being impolite, the innate politician in him, won through.

"Umm, alright give me a second. Rather surprised to meet anyone at all down here. Usually, I'm all alone. Here, I'll give you a hand." An inkling told me he'd rather have kicked me away from the shore and into the water. Maybe I picked up on his own survival instincts, warning him of my deceit. My true intent.

No indecision showed in his eyes nor any fear in his voice. Rather, a feeling of suppressed revulsion, panic even, touched me. Once more, time slowed right down to a standstill. My heart beat so strong it seemed like it must be audible to him. Part of me panicked as I realised the intuition crackling between us broadcast only raw truth. Deep down he knew. Like prey to a crafty predator, tempted to take a drink. Coaxed despite the hairs beginning to stand up on his back. Yet I knew my own senses had been sharpened, honed in combat and duress. To a level of sensitivity far above normal, like Phil's. His mind contained too much clutter. Junk thoughts and avarice mixed with a superiority complex, gave him a constant backdrop of presumed invulnerability. I smiled as he put his binoculars in their case and stepped towards me. Placing them on the ground close by, he stooped to pull on my proffered arm, keeping a yard or so away from the edge.

"Don't worry fella, I'm not going to pull you in!" I said smiling wide. "Here, let me get my elbow on the..." I shuffled around and bullshitted for a few more seconds, to put him off balance as he leant forwards. Moving too swift for him to stand up but slow enough to keep him uncomfortable. Looking at his right knee, grasping his right hand with my own, then he began to straighten up and pull. Allowing him to take my weight, whilst turning to hide my left hand, secured The Crook into position.

An explosion of energy. A lead-filled rubber cosh came from between my legs and into my left hand, whilst jerking Phil forwards with my right. The cosh came down onto Phil's right knee. He went white then crumpled, gasping. He didn't even see it coming. The shock took the wind from him for a moment but he soon drew in a lungful to let out a shrill, anguished scream.

The heavy cosh cut off Phil's noise by smashing his Adam's apple and windpipe with a single crushing blow. Spluttering and twitching, The Crook collapsed to his knees, offering little resistance to being dragged into the canal. Drowning him proved even less of a struggle. All whilst sitting in the little boat. The real problem proved to be dragging the corpse through the water.

The binoculars went around The Crook's head. My intention had been to pull the cadaver over to a thick belt of reeds but it kept snagging on things below the surface. His woollen clothing pulling Phil's corpse under. Time could not be wasted on getting the thing into a prime position. It would be discovered sooner or later anyway. After fifteen minutes splashing through cold water whilst struggling on the slime underfoot, one place along the lonely stretch of canal became as good as another. The clammy remains had to be gotten rid of.

A chunk of reinforced concrete sufficed as an anchor. Convenient protrusions of rebar acting as hooks to attach the body to. I'd found it on a previous occasion, placing it close to the towpath. After pulling the trousers down to knee level to bind the legs together, I entangled the leather strap of the binoculars around the hook, then let the corpse sink to the dingy bottom of the canal. A frigid burial for a cold heart.

———⟫•◆•⟪———

Subsequent moments blur by in my memory. Scuttled the Kayak with a camping axe. Leaving her among the thickest section of reeds felt wasteful, but necessary. Changed clothes to some kept dry in a waterproof rucksack hidden in the kayak. The wet-suit and wind-proofs went in the rucksack. Sliced them to ribbons before weighing the bag down with large stones. A mile or so further along the canal, this also went to the bottom.

Spent the rest of the day in a pub. An expansive place on a crossroads called The Black Greyhound. Well inland, over thirty miles from the Hit. Eating a large dinner, enjoying several pints of stout whilst filling the one-armed bandit with fresh coins. Although remaining discreet, my expenditure alone ensured my face would be remembered. The barmaid took to me, so I asked her out. We agreed to meet two nights later. Choosing to remain *in-situ* following the Hit could be perceived as counter-intuitive. In this case however it made little difference.

Phil's remains came to light following a long search. Police frogmen weren't sent in to scour the canal until eight days after I'd snuffed out his deceitful life. Some effort went into looking for Phil around the little Mere. These factors kept my involvement covered. In the end, his unwarranted reputation and political connections kept the spotlight off murder. The coroner could not determine how the injuries occurred due to the condition of the corpse. A good proportion of the flesh had been eaten away. The face, neck and throat. Foul play could not be ruled out, but a verdict of Accidental Death protected his family from disgrace.

———⟫•◆•⟪———

What had Phil done to cause those men to drown? For all intents and purposes, he worked them to death. The foreman of the crew had been a close friend of Phil's. A new bridge had to be built on the estuary. Plenty more work came Phil's way and he capitalised on it. However, the foreman developed a bout of pneumonia, which had put him off work for a month that year. When he'd returned, the new works were behind schedule. The Crook, always out to impress his overlords, threw time and money at his friend to get a particular task completed which would relieve the situation.

He'd done it too. The foreman friend of Phil's. Worked like a trooper. The accident that killed the men came about because he'd been exhausted. Running on empty, without being fully recovered from the illness. Working long, cold hours on the open shoreline. He miscalculated the tides. The men were surprised by incoming seawater rushing along narrow channels cut between the new abutments. Working on a dark evening, assuming they still had an hour left. The rapid surge of the tidal bore overwhelmed the men before any could react. Battered, swept along and chilled to the bone by the sudden on-rush of cold seawater, they stood little chance. The one survivor, whilst he still lingered in life, had given a graphic account of their ordeal.

According to him; - "The five of us ended up on a sandbank just downstream. Two were injured, one concussed and I was vomiting water. No-one had the strength to make an attempt to swim for the shore. The tide kept rushing past us in a constant flow. It was far too powerful; we couldn't even stand up in it. It was a freezing torrent and the wind just blasted right through our wet clothes. We were all shivering, uncontrolled like. We shouted for help as loud as we could but it was no use."

If anyone did hear their desperate cries, the water had risen so fast nothing could be done in time. Panic gripped the men as the acuteness of the situation bit into their frantic minds. The survivor said he chose to allow the current to carry him up-river. Coming close to drowning himself, instead fortune swept him onto a mud-bank close to the shore, where he'd managed to get a grip on the reeds. The others were not so lucky. All four of their drowned bodies were recovered over subsequent days.

Their families failed to receive any compensation. Phil had washed his hands of any involvement. Instead, he made certain a lower-level manager became the scapegoat. But in the end the local authority made certain the foreman friend of Phil's took the blame, with the individual men being held responsible for their own safety decisions on site. A shameful decision. Five families without Fathers, without the steady income or any recompense. Left to get on with it. Deplorable.

Phil Guy held the ultimate responsibility. He pushed those men to make up time. He waved money under the nose of his sick friend, knowing he needed it. His friend's wife, not even married a year, had been expecting at the time. Phil went on to move ever onwards and upwards. By the time he met me, he'd moved up a notch in the managerial hierarchy. Closer to his goal of becoming a councillor or even Mayor.

No chance of that now.

LONDON CALLING

London. The Big Smoke provided distractions. Although during this time nightmares cursed my sleep. A drowning man kept me awake. Clawing, scrambling for air. Coughing and thrashing the water into a froth. The drowning man of my nightmares did not die easy as Phil Guy had. Not according to my memory.

In these dreams I mocked the man. Taunting. Allowing him to surface, to suck in a breath of the air his body craved. Letting him recover a little, before pushing him back under. Then repeating the process, again and again. Laughing when his coughing became violent, as he inhaled droplets of the thrashed and frothing-white water. But shaken by his face flashing larger and larger before me, becoming like the visage of a giant, whilst I'd shrunk to the scale of a gnat. His face, overwhelming me with its contorted terror. Becoming all I could perceive, blotting out all else. Attempting to scream, instead stifled, unable to make a sound. Transfixed before the enormous flashing face, dwindling as it swelled into monstrous magnitude. Being stuck in a sleep-paralysis induced by such a nightmare, caused my overnight companion to throw water from a vase over me.

"Mary! What the hell are you doing?"

"You were grabbing me, and the sheets, and your soaked!" She protested.

"I bloody well am now!", I griped at her. Mary stood up and threw me a towel from the en-suite.

"You know what I mean. You were burning up, pouring with sweat", she said, a look of concern flicking across her brow.

We were staying at a small hotel in Reading. As mentioned prior, Mary Preston worked for me in a unique secretarial position. I paid her very well to keep the administrative parts of my business in order. She hired accountants and clerks to do the bookkeeping for my various businesses and investments. With some years experience as a clerk in a City of London insurance brokers, Mary knew enough to know if the accountants were being efficient in their work. The arrangement suited me. I trusted her. Mary had proven her integrity numerous times. Her voice, always soft, sprang out from her mouth as a surprised, gasping exclamation.

"Sam Daniels, what on Earth has gotten into you? Nightmares again?"

"Yeah." Struggling to utter this single syllable, now the shock of the cold water had worn off. Someone seemed to have stuffed my head with cotton wool. Clouds of confusion billowed among stodgy, ossified thoughts. Explaining anything at all seemed daunting.

"Listen Mary sweetheart, would you mind ordering us both a pot of coffee? I don't suppose you have a couple of headache tablets?"

"Yes Sam, I have some in my handbag."

"Oh, do you? Thanks Mary, you're an angel."

"My pleasure", she smiled. Wiping the cold sweat off my head, I watched her hips wriggle in the towel she wrapped around herself. Sounds of Mary going about ordering the drinks helped me begin to feel normal. The dream had been disturbing. That night decided it for me. Bestial needs demanded their sacrificial lamb, or guilt and anxiety would bring about insanity.

'There are plenty more Targets out there.'
'I know. Just waiting for me.'
'Your work is never done.'
'Who will be next?'
'Does it matter as long as they're guilty?'
'Not to me.'

THE MOUTH

Reading, being just West of London served well as a base in the South. I'd had family there until old age took them all away. The Home Counties being excellent for cricket and open, rural space, whilst still close to the city. The libraries of Oxford, Banbury, Bicester and Slough became my research centres. In those days, most archives in libraries were available to the public on microfilm.

Eyes soon became tired reading through the machine's little viewing window. Uncomfortable to sit through for any length of time. After a few weeks, no-one suitable appeared in my searches. Meanwhile, a business associate asked me to join him in a four-ball coming up he deemed important for us to win. He wished to impress his prospect. I called my golf coach Pedro, to book a brush-up lesson a few days prior. This is how fate delivered my next Target. A man who had made himself infamous throughout a number of exclusive country clubs of central England.

Mark Walpole. As big a braggart as they come. All slab teeth and hot air. He loved England because he easily became the loudest person in most social scenarios. Despite being Canadian, he exhibited more the archetypal loudmouth Yank behaviour. Always talking for effect. He acted the clown but his humour carried a vehement edge. Insecurity and jealousy drove barbed comments. Always aimed at the weakest in the group. A gross miscreant, in full denial. A fragile ego sheltering behind a façade of volume and bluff. Ingratiating and obsequious towards social superiors, whilst scheming as a viper towards his peers, and being dismissive and indifferent to those he deemed inferior.

⟫•◊•⟪

One bright morning, Pedro and I spent an hour working on my drive. Afterwards we both had time and he accepted my offer to buy him lunch at the clubhouse. Wishing to pick his brains and query him on a couple of courses coming up in my diary, both of which were new to me. As we received drinks and sat awaiting our food, The Mouth spoke so loud, he didn't need pointing out. However, I'd filtered him out as just another idiot. Midway through eating, Pedro leaned forward.

"You see that fool, the loudmouth?" Keeping his voice low whilst gesturing with a fork. He shoved the fork into his mouth and carried on as if he hadn't spoken. I glanced in the direction he indicated.

"The Yank?"

"Yeah, well, no. He's Canadian." Pedro muttered as he chewed.

"Can't really miss him."

Two well-dressed men accompanied The Mouth. He entertained them with some tale but projected himself across the whole room. Not only his voice. His whole persona. A kind way to describe his manner would be 'larger than life'. However, Mark does not deserve such a genial tag. Demanding all the attention, all the time. A walking advert for himself.

"He has a very shady past. He's only over here because his reputation is ruined back in Canada."

"Ahh, I see. This sounds interesting Pedro. How do you know about him?"

"Everyone knows, Sam!" He kept his voice quiet but his Latin passion gave his words fire. "At least, all the professionals do. Obviously, he doesn't tell anyone about it himself. He won't be telling those two chaps there with him, that's for certain." Pedro went on as I took a better glance at the figure behind the voice.

"Well, are you going to tell me then?" I asked, turning back to him. Pedro smiled, took a gulp of his fresh-squeezed orange juice and enlightened me.

"He played professional ice hockey a for a few seasons, in defence. No big deal or anything, not even for a good team from what I've been told. But he had a knee injury and had to give up. So, he moved into coaching. He ran a kid's team for a number of years. They did well under him. One year, his latest team were playing in the nationals. You know, like between the colleges, that kind of thing." Pedro paused to take a drink. Nodding, smiling, keeping my expression agreeable, I responded; -

"Yes, I know. So, the kids must've been college age then? What, seventeen, eighteen?"

"No, no. Fifteen at the most, these kids. You know what they're like in Canada for ice hockey."

"Oh, it's their cricket. No doubt about it. Their main sport."

"Absolutely. So, they're in this final, semi-final or something. They need to travel some distance to another school. But the weather was horrendous."

"Snow and ice?"

"Not so much. More like heavy rain and fog. That's why he thought it was ok to push the driver to drive too fast."

"Don't tell me the driver and he were the only survivors of the crash?"

"No, most of the kids survived. It wasn't the crash that killed them. Not just the crash."

"The weather?" Seemed to be a reasonable query. Pedro's reaction caught me off guard. He looked at me and nodded agreement, but seemed distracted by evil thoughts and he became demonstrative. Eye's narrowed, brow furrowed, mood darkened. The familiar Latin voice thickened, emotion catching in his throat as he spoke. Pedro had three children and a beautiful wife of his own. The way it affected him made me curious.

As I listened, an idea formed, deep in the murderous quarters of my mind. An energising thrill ran through me. Knowing a fresh Target might be being gifted to me by this happenchance sequence of events. To pick him in person, so to speak. Rather than comparing notes on prospects from library archives. To have contact with the man, to suddenly share the same space as a potential Target sent a bolt of energy through me. But I needed to know more.

'How much blame does he carry?'
'That's what I intend to find out.'
'You're enjoying this.'
'Of course. God has delivered him to me.'
'Is that so?'
'It is.'

The query in my mind full of excited anticipation. Willing, almost praying Pedro would tell me what I wanted to hear, before asking him the question. "So, their deaths were his fault?"

"That's what they say. Of course, he just walked away. The coward." Pedro had an annoying habit when talking, as if he expected you to know the rest of what he had to say. Therefore, he needn't say it.

"Walked away? What, from the crash? What do you mean?"

"From the crash, from the enquiry, the kid's parents, their lawyers. Everything, everybody." Pedro's voice affected even more of an Iberian accent when he spoke faster and faster with excitement.

"What about the law, the police?"

"No. He never broke any law. He claimed amnesia. The driver and the kids who survived say he'd put on as much clothing as he could and set off. Told them he was going to fetch help. He left them to die. He turned up at a roadside hotel late that night and booked himself in!" Pedro leaned back in his chair, shaking his head and shrugging his shoulders, arms wide open in a disbelieving gesture. He went on; - "Most people think he expected them all to die. In the morning he came down to the lobby of the hotel claiming amnesia. By this time emergency services had discovered the accident at first light and had saved as many of those kids as they could. The driver happened to be a big man, so he made it through the night despite having a few busted ribs and a broken ankle. All the injured kids, at least, those who'd lost blood, well, basically they died of exposure." He paused to wet his mouth with a sip of tea before getting to the nitty gritty of the sorry tale.

"It was a bad accident Sam, you understand?" I nodded.

"I do understand, Canada is a good country for bad weather. At least, so I've heard. Rough winters. Go on." Pedro nodded back at me to show he knew he had my full attention. The solemnness of the situation he described to me hung heavy on each of his words.

"According to what I've heard it was like a bloody monsoon out there. No weather to be driving through the mountains. Anyway, all these heavy downpours of rain caused flash floods on the road they were on. Their bus hit a flood on the downward curves, going too fast. The driver lost control and crashed straight through the barrier. The bus was wrecked. The kids all got soaked by hail and rain. They couldn't find shelter from the freezing wind. Only by huddling together against the wreckage did any survive. There was nothing else any of them could have done. They were all nearly dead anyway by the time they were found."

"And *he* claimed amnesia? Are you joking? That's bloody ridiculous!" Jerking a thumb towards where the man stood to emphasise my whispered exclamation.

"That's exactly what the parents said. The driver and surviving kids told a different story. Unfortunately, the law had no way to prove he was lying. As soon as he could, he washed his hands of it all and moved over here. To coach golf to middle-aged ladies!"

"Jesus that's a cowardly thing to do. Cold-hearted bastard."

"Isn't he? He has no integrity, no morals. Now he goes around acting like a professional golfer." Pedro finished his tea and took a packet of Rothmans from his jacket, offering me one whilst pulling an ashtray closer to him. After lighting his cigarette, he pushed his chair out a little and swivelled in his seat to sit sideways on. Resting one arm across the back of it, he drew on the Rothmans and scanned the whole room before resting his eye's once more on the subject of our discussion.

"Ok, well look at him. He doesn't exactly pretend to be a true golf pro, to be honest. He doesn't lie about it, not in that way. Not direct. But he's still a fake. His handicap is not great. He would never make it as a pro. Not at any level." He spun back towards me, sucking smoke from the cigarette with enough anger to crease his face permanently, before spitting out the venom he felt towards the man.

"A damned fake with a nasty secret in his closet!" Pedro sneered. Squinting his brown eyes. The level of animosity surprised me. He really did not like this man.

We carried on talking but I didn't garner anymore significant details out of him. I didn't have to. He'd told me plenty. More than enough. My thoughts turned to how these things Pedro told me might be verified. It would not be as straight forward as visiting a library. But our following exchanges melted from my attention as a most fantastic feeling swept up from my feet. Pure excitement. I had to move, shuffling and fidgeting in the chair to cover the shivers going through me. Pedro had just revealed my next Target.

VIOLENCE TO ORDER

Business issues and charity dinners kept me in London following Pedro's revelations. For a number of months. At weekends often staying over at Mary's place. A compact yet desirable Georgian terraced house in Knightsbridge. A property I'd gifted to her several years earlier.

During the week, South London tended to be my favourite place to find a hotel or guest house. For family reasons, many summers of my youth having been shared with cousins on an uncle's small-holdings by Burgess Park. Down along the Old Kent Road. Attending football matches between the London clubs, as we had back in those halcyon days, when not playing among the bomb craters still left over from the Blitz.

Always guaranteed to be exciting events. A complete contrast to the quiet of a five-day test match at Lords. Enjoying a few beers in the Golden Lion before attending a game at The Den amongst the Millwall faithful produced plenty of opportunity to vent some of my ever-simmering anger and frustrated bloodlust. Shouting at the players, the referee or the linesman allowed for an intriguing range of vitriolic abuse to relieve a little the spite. But the culture of violence at football matches drew me in like a moth to a flame. Although my murderous activities were far more satisfactory, the mob mentality and sheer chaos of 1970's football violence excited my senses. Close enough to the level of military combat to sate my aggressive tendencies, on a number of occasions.

At one such juncture outside London Bridge station I got hurt, cut by some chap with a hidden blade. Nothing serious. Just a slice along the forearm. But the pain, his weapon and the blood threw me into combat mode. A couple of Millwall boys hauled me off or I may well have killed the sly Chelsea yob right there. I'd disarmed and floored the bloke, before proceeding to strangle him with his own shirt-sleeve. He went limp before they pulled me away. Blood from the gash in my arm covered the pair of us. Police turned up and proceeded to wade in and arrest people.

With help and good luck, I avoided being caught. Too close for comfort though. Last thing I needed were the CID snooping around my life. After this particular incident, concentrating on planning my next murder took precedence. Trouble at football matches gave me an outlet for the aggression, but I never felt any great hatred for the thugs we fought against. Although it did release some of the mania, always lurking within.

Bloodlust, the desire to inflict violence. These represented one facet. However, my desires were more complex. Longing to know the sanction of retribution. To be the Wrath of God. To take life from someone who had forsaken their right to live. To put to death and feel vindicated for doing so. These were my needs. Drunken brawling and knife fights helped provide adrenaline for my addiction to it, but fell far short of replacing the rush which came after the successful execution of my homicidal yearnings.

This latest Hit intrigued my mind. Occupying my thoughts whenever I relaxed from business interests. The Mouth would be a challenge. Yet right from the start, the whole thing went as well as it could. I felt Destiny at work. My intention to kill had Divine Blessing.

DIGGING FOR GUILT

S ubstantiating the information provided by Pedro proved easier
than anticipated. Whilst in London, I discovered a way to hire
a private detective in the city of Vancouver. Hired using an alias, of
course. Nothing in particular made me choose Vancouver. Pedro
hadn't mentioned any city or town when he'd told me about The
Mouth. Asking him further about the matter was not an option.

Vancouver came to mind, so that became the place to start. A
new account in a small bank under the same alias had to be set up
in order to wire the private detective a generous advance payment.
Back then, pretending to be someone else couldn't have been much
easier. Cash helped. Greasing wheels being the way things were
done. No-one asked questions. Money talked its own language and
kept its own secrets.

Arrangements were made via telegraph, airmail and telephone.
Pretending to have a connection to distant family, playing a relative
of one of the bereaved parents. By these means, within another
month I had learnt as much about the case as my source in Canada
could find. Indeed, the information proved accurate. Pedro's
account covered most of it. Dennis, the private eye in Vancouver,
told me in plain English during an overseas 'phone call. Acting
as my alias, Mr Turner, at a small hotel in Crawley. My home
for the night, prior to a meeting Mary had arranged for me at
Gatwick airport with a well-connected investor from Austria the
following day.

'Mr Turner' requested an international connection to
Vancouver. Not a common request in those days at such a small

hotel. However, the staff already knew I had plenty of cash. After booking the most expensive room and food available, they would jump at the opportunity. The charge on my bill would likely far exceed the actual cost of the call. No matter. All this assured my privacy would be respected.

My craving intensified. Consumed by the need for Mark to be guilty. The urge to slay pushed at the civility of rational thoughts. Fraying the edges of consideration. I prayed to God Pedro's tales about The Mouth were true. It never occurred to me at the time this also meant wishing eight kids had died due to this man's failings. No consideration for the eight families whose sons did not return from a simple school outing.

The line scratched and crackled, but Dennis' voice came through clear enough. After exchanging greetings, I asked him for the rawest version of events. He got straight into it; -

"According to the driver and the surviving boys, Mark Walpole had argued with the driver, forcing him to travel too fast as they struggled to make the schedule. The driver lost control on a long mountain descent in heavy rain. The bus crashed through the barrier and rolled to a stop down a small but steep ravine."

"How many died in the crash? It sounds like it was pretty bad."

"Now that's the thing Mr Turner. You see, although those eight boys got seriously injured, none of them died from the wreck itself."

"So, what happened? How come Mark was alright?"

"He was hurt but he got off lightly. Only minor bumps and scrapes. The driver's report is obviously the most coherent. He said at the time that within minutes of them pulling the boys together and assessing the situation, Mark realised only he still had the ability to climb back up onto the road. So, he chose to leave them."

"Perhaps he left with good intentions," I offered, but Dennis wouldn't commit.

"I wouldn't know about that, Mr Turner."

"Maybe, struggling in the conditions himself, he felt the others stood no chance of making it until morning anyway."

"Well, that's one way of looking at it. Most everybody involved with the case blames him. He should have reported the accident when he got to that hotel. That's what everyone said at the time and they're still saying it."

"But he went for amnesia, eh?"

"No way to prove it, one way or the other." Dennis noted.

"No, I suppose not." I agreed.

"But no-one bought it either. He lost a lot of friends after all that. Even his family cut him off."

"He has family?"

"An older sister, she hasn't had anything to do with him in years."

"Once she'd realised he was lying, I suppose."

"Probably. Being associated with him became an embarrassment for anybody who did know him. You know, due to the stigma of the case. The publicity. The news covered the story for weeks. After the hearing he couldn't get the kind of work he wanted over here, so he moved over to the UK."

"When was that?"

"Three years ago."

"And he's built a business up for himself over here?"

"As far as I can tell, yes. He offers his services as a golf tutor and a personal trainer, for a good fee too, from what I can gather."

"Does he conduct his business all over the country?" My intention being to find out where Mark lived and worked, but discretion had to be employed. After all, within a few months the Target would be a corpse. This conversation and the alias I had assumed could be looked into.

"I don't know about that. I can tell you he tends to be between Coventry and Oxford. His business is registered in Oxfordshire but he also has a Coventry listed number in the phone book there."

"Thank you, Dennis, you've been a great help. I really appreciate your efforts."

"No problem, thank you for the business Mr Turner."

Replacing the phone receiver, a great feeling overcame me. Another Hit to begin working on. Although, tracking Mark's habits proved neither straightforward nor easy at all.

Age and maturity have since cleared my vision. Enough to realise how out of control I'd become by that time. The urge to kill had complete mastery over me.

'To kill is a sin.'
'Not when they have forfeited their right to live.'
'Who decides that?'
'God does. I am his justice.'
'How so?'
'God made me into what I am.'
'And what is that?'
'His Wrath on Earth.'

Divine intervention must have caused me to discover this Target. For our paths to have crossed on that day, at that time, with Pedro and I sharing a rare lunch together, could only mean one thing. Such a random sequence of coincidences showed proof my work must be ordained.

It took a while to detail any sort of reliable routine for The Mouth's activities. His appointments having the tendency to be either on the whim of himself or his client. Over time, predicting his movement on certain days became accurate. From there, a strategy began to take form. However, he had a tendency to overrun his appointments, then dash around making up for lost time. Planning the Hit became a serious headache. He never stayed alone for long at all.

In the end the method chosen involved sabotaging Mark's vehicle. Being able to predict where his car would be on certain days. Tampering with his car unseen would be child's play. Yet this would not ensure death. I had to damage his car, in a fatal way. When certain he would be driving alone, on a journey involving open roads. He liked to speed between towns and golf courses in a saloon version of Jaguar's XJ6.

Obtaining an owner's manual for the Jag delivered insights. Sabotaging the brakes seemed to be a viable option but not easy. Risking the possibility of the problem being discovered before getting up too much speed. The damage or incapacitation would have to increase gradually until a fatal accident occurred. In a single journey. At night. Setting myself those parameters gave me confidence in the Hit. Knowing it could work sat at the heart of my creativity.

Hours spent studying the manual paid off. Hitting the brakes alone didn't convince me. The suspension and steering would have to be tampered with too, but how? Without being seen? Without him suspecting a problem and preventing the accident? Time became my best asset. To cover every angle. Winter had to be the season of the Hit. God put me on this Earth to ensure it happened.

'Ah yes, God.'

'Yes. God.'

Before the Hit could be finalised, Mark moved house, to live in Ashby-de-la-Zouch, Leicestershire. This helped. He'd have further to travel to his usual haunts in Oxfordshire and the Home Counties. Although something irked me. The car. Could I do the necessary sabotage when the time came? When it mattered most, on the heady night of the Hit? A solution occurred to me after a day spent at Trent Bridge, watching Notts beat the Yorkshire team in a wonderful one-day Test Match.

Acquire the same model Jaguar, hire a garage space and practice accessing the car's vitals. Hour after hour, time after time. When I got good at it enough to be able to close my eyes, I'd practice fitting my devices with wet hands, in the cold. With soaked clothes on. Anything to make it as uncomfortable as possible. Because the night of the Hit would be full of foul weather. It had to be.

Autumn arrived bringing wilful force and bluster. Storms across England knocked trees over and flooded roads. Good omens for dire purposes. The Mouth regaled and entertained posh English knobs who viewed him as little more than a colonial clown. He fawned around, all flashy teeth and clever wit. Falling over himself to help the ladies with a coat or golf bag. Later, speaking in low-tones, man-talking among thick cigar smoke in the Men's Lounge with their husbands. Mark knew how to charm alright. Yet all his smarmy efforts amounted each time to little more than a handful of prospects. However, despite lacking the best golfing skills, he could motivate and his flattery provided good company for the vacuous types who hired him. He knew how to make them feel important. To some people, he seemed a great guy. Life and soul of the party. Jolly old Mark, always made people around him laugh. Yet his accusatory secret haunted him, represented by my scrutineering presence.

EITHER WAY

"*...i*ncluding *heavy rain and sleet, with fog across most parts of England and Wales throughout the night and well into the morning.*" The radio station's weatherman detailed the ominous conditions forecast for the weekend.

"*My word Mike, I think I'll be staying indoors until this thing blows over. Doesn't look like good conditions at all for travel.*" The host said, prompting weatherman Mike to help fill in more airtime.

"*That's right Tony, icy roads, rain, wind and hail; - I certainly wouldn't want to get caught out in it. The AA and RAC have both advised their members not to drive at all unless it is absolutely necessary.*" Mike replied.

"*And how long do you expect this to last Mike?*"

"*Right through the weekend Tony, it may get a little less wild as far as the wind is concerned but we're in for heavy rain for a few more days yet, I'm afraid. My advice is to keep listening to the bulletins and keep up to date with the weather, if you really need to be out in it. Otherwise, I wouldn't bother going very far at all.*"

"*Well, I'm sure our listeners here on Thames Valley Radio will be heeding those wise words Mike and keeping their cars on the driveway. The local pubs within walking distance, so you've all got nothing to worry about!*"

"*Sounds like the perfect solution to me Tony, just remind them to take an umbrella.*"

"*I'm sure they heard you there. Well, thank you Mike and we'll have another report from you just before Midnight. Moving on, here's the latest hit from one of my oldest favourites...*"

I clicked the radio off. Having served its purpose of confirming the forecasts of a storm front bringing downpours and high winds across central England. Right where I needed it. With a good chance of black ice and hail to boot on higher ground. Perfect.

Something different for this Target. Estrangement from the gore and horror. Sabotage allowed Mark an element of chance. If he didn't get in the car for some reason, or stopped the journey before reaching the point of no return, there wouldn't be another attempt. The Mouth had come to me through sheer chance, it felt right to leave him in the hands of Lady Luck.

Mark had a big night planned. An exclusive party at this remote country club, situated on the edge of the Cotswolds. The place being a Tudoresque mock-up, rebuilt on the grounds of the previous mansion, destroyed by fire in 1855. Occupying a long ridgeline, patched with fields, separated by knots of woodlands and leafy glades. During the 1930's the owner had the golf course built into the landscape. Since which time, anywhere flat and close enough to the clubhouse had been cleared and rolled with Tarmacadam, to create space for the growing number of clients and members vehicles.

The party had begun early and went on until after Midnight. Giving me hours of darkness to work in. The downside being the parking. Uneven ground caused by gradients and tree roots all made the conditions less than perfect for working under a car, most of all in the dark. Having prior knowledge of this prompted me to come fore-armed. Those long hours of disciplined practice came into effect. The problem of sabotaging his car in a way guaranteed to work had consumed me.

In the end, it worked like a charm. Small containers made of simple plastics, installed in key positions and set to react to precise input. A few rod connectors primed and pushed on them to deliver certain amounts of acid to specific places around the car's engine compartment and chassis. Others would release acid each time he hit a set number of revs or speed while yet more were triggered by heavy braking. Simple springs and connectors, made bespoke to the car, composed the skeleton of the system.

Using water, the system had worked to perfection on the Jaguar I'd bought, after some practise. A few small snips and saw-cuts here and there and the equipment fit snug around the engine compartment and chassis of Mark's Jaguar. Another few cuts and abrasions to a few more vital parts of the vehicle, to make sure. The acid would take a little while into the journey to have any effect. But within a short time of the last of the acid being released, he would lose all control of the car. The engine would accelerate to full revs, the brakes would fail to respond, the gears would stick, and the steering wheel would spin in his hands.

———◆———

I remained lurking, wanting to watch Mark drive off. Waiting in the cold went by slow, eroding my patience. After Midnight worry crept in. Other guests returned to their cars, laughing and rushing from the damp and cold. Perhaps he'd gotten too drunk or been given a lift? However, he turned up as the party dwindled. A little worse for wear but sober enough to avoid the puddles in his brown-suede winkle-pickers. My heart beat harder with anticipation. Mark started the car, let it warm up a few minutes, clearing his windscreen before pulling out and shooting off down the club's exit drive. Engine roaring loud. Driving hard into the ferocious night.

———◆———

All due respect to Jaguar and that old XJ of Mark's. The car took him a good few miles up the A46, the old Foss Way, before The Mouth had met his doom, killed upon impact, the elements playing their part in his death. Low visibility and fog patches caused a tailback he'd ploughed straight into the back of. Without any sabotage, the accident could have happened anyway. Heavy flooding delayed already stretched emergency services on that ruthless night. His accident didn't get attended to for over forty minutes.

Mark smashed the Jaguar into the back of a stationary lorry. The driver had a CB radio set and sent out a message for help. Back in those days at that hour of night, making a telephone call could be difficult. On that particular stretch of road, no public telephones existed for miles. No emergency phones, not even a pub. Emergency services pronounced Mark dead at the scene. I wondered if he'd suffered before he died.

'Could he have survived the impact?'
'He may have still been conscious.'
'Did he try to prevent the crash?'
'He must have hit the brakes.'
'That wouldn't have helped him by that point in his journey.'
'Far from it.'

Police reports noted a lack of skid-marks, suggesting he hadn't applied his brakes. I knew different. The acid had worked. No-one bothered to examine the car in detail. No one had to. My assembly of rods, tubes and springs destroyed, mere bits among the larger wreckage. The damage from the acid would be obvious to a professional mechanic, but Mark's old Jag ended up taking her secrets to the junkyard.

PART TWO

COVERT COMMUNICATIONS

T hings changed once 1976 ended. Work on the next Target took
me into new territory. Involving a greater element of danger.
Despite the success of these endeavours, that year of endless summer
and plagues of Ladybirds characterises the end of my own hunting's
"Happy Time".

This modification began in the New Year. An indirect result of
the death of Mark Walpole. The wagon driver's CB radio caught my
imagination. Although this fact hadn't come to my attention until
the local radio reported details of the accident the following day. I
had to drive up to the vicinity to be able to receive the stations local
to the crash, in order to find out Mark's fate. National news had
much bigger stories to report.

The idea of Citizens Band radio fascinated me. The laws
governing their usage were restrictive for serious operators. Due to
this, the lorry driver chose to remain incognito to the police. Yet
he still managed to contact someone who passed the message along
to someone else, until it had reached the emergency services. I felt
drawn to the fact that the initial communication had happened
outside the reach of the law.

These wagon drivers were using two-way radio sets to talk to
each other. As I discovered, users had a unique code and manner
of speech. My investments at the time involved haulage. Whilst at
the Plaza hotel in the centre of Nottingham in January, on the spur
of the moment, I had a call made to Mary in London. The time
being almost seven in the evening, well past business hours. Hoping
she would be at home in Knightsbridge, time ticked away, static

crackled from the hotel telephone's earpiece, until the operators voice came through to say we were connected. The earpiece clicked, announcing the operator had dis-connected and we could talk in private.

"Good evening Mary."

"Hello Sam, how lovely to hear from you! Is everything ok?"

"Yes, everything's fine, thank you. Listen, I need you to find the number for the manager of the haulage firm I own. It's based in Chester."

"Ahem. You own two haulage firms Sam, neither of which are based in Chester. However, one of them *is* based in Crewe, which *is* in Cheshire. Close."

Mary's sardonic smile flew into my mind's eye. She loved a chance to prove how perfect and invaluable her services were. "That's the one, he'll do."

"Would you like me to find the number of the other firm?" She knew I didn't. This being her way of opening up an opportunity to learn more, knowing full well nothing would come of it. She wanted to keep me on the phone as long as possible. For me, it provided an opportunity to demonstrate my true affections for her. Even if only from afar, in the tone of my voice and the polite, respectful manner of my speech.

"No, no thank you Mary, that won't be necessary right now."

"You sure? It's really no trouble at all."

"I'm sure, just the number for the Crewe firm, I know that chap a little better."

"Okay Sam but I can't really help you until the morning. Not unless you want me to drive over to the office right now?"

"Your tone suggests you know the answer to that question Mary." I observed without judgement. "No, of course it isn't urgent enough to warrant me calling you up at home." Pausing for effect, I listened to her breathing on the other end of the line. She remained silent, waiting for me to speak. "It's nice for me to hear your voice, Mary."

"Well thank you Sam, that's very sweet. You should know I don't mind you calling me at any time."

"Really? You don't have any plans for tonight then? No date with some lucky chap?"

"Sam Daniels! I'm all alone here, and quite happy that way, thank you very much."

"Just teasing Mary. But I wouldn't know what to do if someone swept you off your feet and took you away from me."

"I'm not going anywhere Sam. No chance of being swept off my feet by anyone! My feet are firmly on the ground, as you know."

"That's very reassuring to hear. I couldn't live my life the way I do without your help."

"Oh, I know Sam, don't worry about that!" She chuckled down the phone. "Anything else, only I have food in the oven waiting to be eaten."

"I'd like that number before noon tomorrow, if possible, thanks. You can reach me here at the hotel." We ended the call with overt affection and simmering, latent passion in our words.

⟫◆⟪

Who better to call? Mike Tansley, the owner of the firm in Crewe and I had met a few years prior at a gala dinner event in Chester. We were introduced by an investor associate. Mike would have the answers to my questions.

Mary called to give me the number before nine-fifteen the following morning. I replaced the receiver and rang room service to order a coffee, before dialling. Mike's secretary put me straight through to him after ascertaining my identity.

"Good morning Mr Daniels," Mike said, sounding troubled, worried, "this is a surprise. How can I help?"

"Good morning Mike. Please, call me Sam. I appreciate the surprise this must be. But this isn't about business. I'm after picking your brains for a few minutes, if you have time? I can call a little later if you're busy."

"No, it's fine Sam. Now is good. This afternoon I'll be busy kicking a few arses, got to keep the workforce sharp." His ragged guffaw rattled from the earpiece. Then, inhaling on a cigar, it sounded like. I could swear he leant back in his chair before replying; "What do you want to know?"

"Tell me about these CB radios the wagon drivers are using now. Do your drivers use them?"

"Well, that's about the last question I expected you to ask, Sam." He laughed a little more but my silence brought him to the realisation of my earnestness. He coughed, then spoke. This time his voice had lost all trace of humour. "As far as I know, a lot of drivers have taken to using CB radios now. They're useful. We can't really stop the drivers doing so and why would we even bother trying to? If the police catch them at it, they're on their own. We don't know anything about it." Feeling my question had gotten his heckles up, or at least the subject touched a nerve, I tried to placate him. Lowering my tone and slowing the delivery of my words.

"Ok Mike, I see. I didn't realise CB is illegal."

"Not exactly illegal Sam, depends which frequency they use and the power of their equipment."

"Hmm, more interested in the technology Mike. I'm a bit of a radio hack, well, used to be."

"Ham radio, all that?" He sounded relieved yet still irritated. It seemed to me Mike knew nothing technical about much at all but didn't want me to realise it.

"Yes, kind of. CB fascinates me Mike, only recently heard of it. I thought I could use one when I'm out and about in the hills, in the Land-Rover. I'm interested in finding out the range of them. Mobile two-way radio for the public is a debatable idea I suppose. Plenty of dubious types out there."

"Yeah, all sorts of nastiness could be done. Everyone's anonymous. No telephone numbers, no bills to pay either."

"But how does anyone know who they're talking to?"

"They don't. They all use nicknames. They have a special way of talking to each other, so they know when it's an outsider speaking."

"What, like a code? With secret names?" This piece of information intrigued me.

"Yep", he answered. I had to let this sink in before responding.

"Wow, no wonder it's dodgy."

"Perhaps. Like I said though Sam, not exactly illegal. But the police don't always approve of them. Drivers who use a CB set are more likely to be pulled over. Then the coppers could find anything, bald tyre, loose load. No-one wants that. My drivers know the score. If they attract bad luck, they're on their own", the phone went quiet for a moment. Sounds of the cigar being re-lit crackled down the line into my ear before he went on. "I hope you can appreciate how I can't really help you much more Sam."

"I know, it's fine Mike."

"But I hope I've been helpful. Don't want you to think you've wasted your time."

"Not at all. You've been a great help. I understand plenty more now, thanks. I appreciate it."

Answers, but not technical specifications. The availability of specific crystals to be used in certain sets, the bandwidth, range and power available for transmission. Knowledge which had to be sought out.

Specialised magazines provided the know-how to create a basic set up. Facilitating my purchase of a cheap and simple CB set and listening to conversations in an old Series VI Morris Oxford. One of the British cars at the time inspired by, and designed at the Pininfarina coachbuilders based in Turin. The way CB users spoke to each other imparted insider knowledge. As the reach of my listening ear stretched, so did my curiosity in the uses of this form of communication.

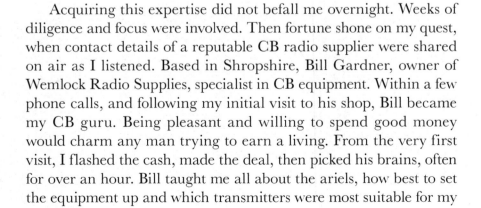

Acquiring this expertise did not befall me overnight. Weeks of diligence and focus were involved. Then fortune shone on my quest, when contact details of a reputable CB radio supplier were shared on air as I listened. Based in Shropshire, Bill Gardner, owner of Wemlock Radio Supplies, specialist in CB equipment. Within a few phone calls, and following my initial visit to his shop, Bill became my CB guru. Being pleasant and willing to spend good money would charm any man trying to earn a living. From the very first visit, I flashed the cash, made the deal, then picked his brains, often for over an hour. Bill taught me all about the ariels, how best to set the equipment up and which transmitters were most suitable for my purposes.

"Rack it up Bill, spare no expense."

"I don't want you to think I'm taking advantage, Sam."

"Behave! I love spending money on the best products. As my grandma used to say, 'buy cheap, buy twice.'"

"I can't argue with wise words like those, very true. So, let's see, you want me to increase the range and power of the set you have in your Oxford out there, as well as an entire new set-up for a static station? For your home?" He asked.

"Absolutely."

"Would a large static ariel be a problem where you live?" He gestured to an advertisement poster on his wall displaying a girl standing next to an outbuilding of some sort with an ariel of about twenty-five feet tall bolted onto the ridge.

"In what way?"

"Some people get complaints from neighbours due to the size of the larger ariel."

"Neighbours aren't a problem, but there are some pretty big trees surrounding the place."

"The best thing to do there then is take the tallest extension to the ariel we stock. That will put you up as high as forty feet if you need it to, but you'll have to use our largest reinforced brackets and bolts, as well as an eighth of an inch steel cable to anchor it down with, just in case of high winds."

"Do you stock those?

"I have the bracket which is good for the ariel and a looped cable but I don't stock the strongest bolts available. If you're going to mount the full extent of the ariel, I'd recommend using them. Most of my customers want the rig-mounted gear, if you get me. Static stations are only just beginning to take off, since word of them in the states came over. But you could pick up the right bolts at any decent hardware store."

"Good enough. Do you know of any?"

"There's an old fella runs a store in Normanton off the main road to Shrewsbury. You could try him."

"Nice one Bill. I'll do just that, once we've settled up here."

Sure enough, the hardware store run by an old-time gentleman in a discreet Shropshire village provided heavy duty steel bolts to anchor the aerial extension. Good old Bill.

———◈———

Bill's advice and equipment elevated my abilities for using the CB to best effect. Although I'd lied about the static station and the large ariel. Those went into storage until I had a place to set them up. A Ford Transit van proved more suitable than the Morris to equip with the improved CB gear. These changes brought the reward of a strong, clear signal. The reduction of static making listening in a fascination, rather than a chore. Becoming enjoyable. The diversion of CB radio brought relief from the mania. By focusing on cramming my brain with knowledge on the subject, as opposed to concentrating on the next kill.

WHO'S WHO?

Most CB conversations were irrelevant, but still offered a source of information. I had a need to make trusted acquaintances outside London. CB radio offered at least some measure of anonymity. As ever, cash greased the necessary wheels. A contact using the handle 'Pele' became my man to go to for Black Market information. My illicit activities were consuming as many as three vehicles each year. Cars and vans, used daily, whilst working on a Hit in a particular town or city. After my bloody work had been done, these motors had to be sold or scrapped at the earliest opportunity.

Cars weren't my only form of transport. First-Class rail travel took me from city to city, as well as to and from London. Yet vehicles allowed unparalleled freedom for stalking each Target whilst seeming to have other purposes. The problem being that selling or scrapping cars following a Hit presented its own issues and potential pitfalls.

Intuition made me wary of using regular scrapyards around the country. A stranger like myself would draw attention, attempting to get rid of a nice motor in good condition. Besides, people noticed me everywhere I went. A phenomenon I'd long been used to. Well-dressed, non-local accent. Turning up with a nice car to be scrapped could prove conspicuous. The off-chance of my type of car being connected to any possible investigation put me off. Although some of the vehicles were used during a Hit, none were ever connected to the Target in any other way. But regular scrap-dealers were out, I could not be too careful.

This entailed having cars to sell following each Hit. Which would coincide with a wave of business meetings, pre-arranged by the ever faithful and ultra-competent Mary. Often all of this happened within a few weeks. Due to these factors, many of the motors were sold for cash, to a dealer in South London called Carl Harris. One of the Millwall faithful. A man who could be trusted to ask no questions and sell each car on within a week or two, for the right price. Carl always welcomed me with big smiles, rubbing his podgy hands together because he knew he'd be getting a bargain.

"Awight Sam! Another one, eh? I dunno where you've been in this thing and I don't care as long as you'll let me take her off yer 'ands for two 'undred quid!" Being the usual manner of verbiage during his greeting. Carl made it easy enough. However, selling cars for cash felt incongruous whilst in London, attending investment group meetings and other business conferences.

————⊙————

At my request, 'Pele' found me a middle-man. Only she turned out to be a middle-woman. Val Frobisher, who came to my attention through mutual connections she and 'Pele' had in the CB community. 'Pele' put the two of us in touch through CB, to facilitate my need for a discreet method of scrapping cars. Destroying them outright. Having them crushed and removed from existence. Over a short time, Val and I built a rapport.

We chatted about technical CB issues concerning different transmitters, etc. As often as not, she used a static location. A base-station, in her home. Other times speaking from a set mounted in her car. However, semi-legal signal boosters and other enhanced equipment enabled Val, using the handle - 'Vienna Rose', to speak with people much further afield from home than any mobile set could.

'Pele' informed me 'Vienna Rose' used CB for giving occasional coded messages to particular individuals. These would refer to purposes which she didn't want the police to have any knowledge of. She handled vehicles which had been used for all manner of nefarious activities. It took a good deal of time and trust-building effort before becoming fully acquainted with Val Frobisher. For months I only knew her as 'Vienna Rose.' But then, her and 'Pele' only knew me as my CB handle; - 'Dynamite', before getting to know me as Dan Turner.

ALIAS ENTANGLEMENTS

My alias Dan Turner. The only point of contact for everyone connected to this chapter of my life. A parallel chapter to my actual, real life. Dan Turner developed an involvement with Val through her connections to the underworld of Lincolnshire and East Anglia. Through our CB rapport, 'Pele' set up a meeting with 'Vienna Rose', by offering good money, above her asking price, for a car to be crushed, no questions asked. The car, a 1970 Opel Manta in need of some repair, had in fact been in storage for two years. Only requiring care and attention but had to be sacrificed for this purpose.

A true fringe-dweller, Val Frobisher played a pivotal role in my life. Though she never really knew it. The man Val thought she knew did not exist. She only ever knew Dan Turner. A husk, a shadow of a man. Her entry into my life began the dramatic sequence of events which took me into the next phase of it. Which in turn brought me here. Writing this account of my murderous practises during those drastic years.

A hefty amount of cash ensured no questions could ever be answered. With Val, no trace of the vehicle remained. Yet her services were not easy to come by. Just a mention of a rumour heard, about a woman going by a particular handle, who could dispose of 'tainted' cars. The beauty of CB radio being anonymity for the user. Although technically possible, for the police to track down a particular signal required practical implications beyond their capabilities, if not their interest, back in those days. CB being still such a marginal activity, regulating its operators had not yet been deemed of high necessity.

———◆◆◆———

What I first heard about Val came from 'Pele'. To begin with, via coded phrases over the CB airwaves. Later he gave me more details, during one of the occasions we had breakfast together. At a motel on a stretch of the A1 in Nottinghamshire. "Well Dan," he said as we awaited the food, "she's got her own yard, that's where she crushes the motors."

"Does she? That makes it nice and simple. Whereabouts is it? Do you know?"

"Yeah, well, no; - but I do know roughly. Somewhere on a canal-side out in Norfolk, twenty miles East of King's Lynn, more or less", he asserted.

"Any idea how big her yard is?"

"The fellow I spoke to, he paid her to get rid of a couple of cars. He told me she has a good-sized yard for such a private place. Used to be her dad's, he was well known around there."

"Sounds perfect."

"Although he did tell me she also has cars stored in empty lorry trailers for security and to keep them out of the weather. Apparently, there's an old lock-keepers cottage on the site, but she spends most of her time living on a narrowboat."

———◆◆◆———

Via CB, Val invited me to meet in Lincolnshire to dispose of the Opel. After dealing with business at the greasy table of an oily roadside café, we both felt comfortable. Enough for a suggestive rapport to develop. Val ordered coffee and sat opposite me on the red Gingham-patterned Formica table. An accomplice came along with her. A large, bald man in his fifties. He took the keys for the Manta without a flicker of sound or emotion. He left and then appeared walking across our window, got into the car and drove away in much the same manner.

We both watched this. Then Val turned to me with a grin and asked; - "So, where you from then Dan?" Before sipping her steaming coffee.

"Oh, you know, here and there," I answered with a smile.

"Here and there, eh? Never been to that place, heard a lot about it though," she winked.

"How about you?" I countered, shifting the emphasis away from myself. "Pele told me you live on a canal somewhere. You always lived on the canals?" Experience had taught me that most people's favourite subject is themselves and their own acquired knowledge, naturally enough.

"Certainly have Dan. Canal Gypsy me. When I was little, we were over in Staffordshire and sometimes the Black Country. Dad moved us over to Norfolk when I got to about fourteen."

"Oh yeah, what about school, did you have to keep changing them then?"

"No, dad never bothered sending me after we moved. Had too much work for me to do around his boats."

"Doesn't seem to have left you lacking much though", I winked and smiled. Val smiled back and gave a chuckle before replying;

"I learnt to read well enough. And once you can read, you can pretty much learn anything you want to."

"Couldn't agree more. So, you never felt the urge to leave?"

"Leave?" She asked, surprise raising the volume of her voice. Then, lower; - "What, like leave home?"

"Yeah, you know, once you'd grown old enough?"

"Didn't really ever have the option Dan. By the time I was seventeen dad was already very badly ill. He weren't able to do a lot of the things he was used to doing. He never really did adjust to the fact. I had to stay around and help him get by. My help and presence didn't improve his temper much. Especially in the winter months. But if I hadn't of done it for him, no-one else would've."

Val spoke much softer now. Emotion pushing through her words. I began to appreciate Val Frobisher could be a rare type of person. One of real substance and integrity. Our eyes met as she lifted her mug again and we both recognised a connection had been made. We knew we would meet again.

⟫◆⟪

Months later, Val's place turned out to be about as rural as it could be. Well under the radar of any serious crime squad. Val's connection to the underworld came through her notorious brother, Sean. However, his existence remained unknown to me until far too late.

All three of our fates, Val's, Sean's and my own intertwined. With disastrous consequences. To this day, I can't decide who came out of it worst. But the fault lay heavy at my feet. By my pretence and deception. Otherwise, our paths could never have crossed in such an intimate and compulsive manner.

This first contact opened the door. My next opportunity to hire Val's unique services and get to know her better came months later, within days of killing a pair of Targets. My first 'brace' of Targets, perhaps would be the proper way to phrase it. Although the double-header had never been my intention, nor had such thoughts even occurred to me. I remember thinking, as the plan first entered my mind, how Fate has such a dark and unpredictable sense of humour.

TWO FOR ONE

'Kill two birds with one stone.'
'I intend to.'
'You should.'
'I have to.'

The plan grew on me, as the opportunity manifested itself. Whilst under surveillance, one Target exposed another. Martin Alsop, the man who appeared on the news bulletins when staying in Durham stalking The Scruff, appeared in the life of another Target. It transpired that Martin's media-exposed hearing at York crown court several years prior had come to naught. The corrupt, smug bastard walked away scot-free. Exonerated of all charges. Connections and influence once more kept the guilty free from rightful custodial internment.

Not one, but two young, foreign women in Martin's employ had disappeared. Two years apart. The second girl, from the Netherlands, turned up buried in a woodland off the A1 in Lincolnshire. No-one ever knew what became of the first girl, a Norwegian aged only twenty. Martin claimed to know nothing, yet certain facts had aroused the suspicion of detectives. After a lengthy investigation, charges brought against him led to the crown court appearance. A cunning lawyer and back-room negotiations ensured not only his freedom, but acquittal of all charges.

Martin had used his wealth to attract the co-operation of local newspapers many times prior to his hearing. Although only ever to highlight his own interests. Courting the media is a double-edged sword. He had his detractors long before any allegations ever hit the local news. Martin turned up whilst I had my next Target, Brian Vickerstaff, under close observation. Out of the blue, in walks Martin.

As with Mark Walpole, being around simultaneous to Pedro and I, this had to be Divine Intervention. Impossible to ignore. Realising the two of them were connected, lust for the challenge of the deed took over. To forego this opportunity would be a sin. An impulse drove me to figure out a method to kill these two men, together. A work I would undertake in honour of this gift of opportunity fortune had presented me with.

COMPELLED

The compulsion to slaughter underpinned all my other activities. Removing myself from people in order to do so. Keeping business partners amenable, but at arm's length. Although attending functions, such as balls and dinners on occasion, my social life did not exist. The women who occupied my time were all short-term acquaintances.

Treating these women as well as possible. Sparing no expense whilst out wining and dining but keeping them at a distance, as far as romance went. Which often wasn't so simple in practise as it is to write down. A few hearts were broken along the way. This is the problem when you behave agreeably and have the means to spoil your dates. They desire the security they perceive in these actions. Other women who shared my time were hired escorts, beautiful, discreet, well-mannered. Bringing an air of business along with their pleasure. Useful for some of the more exclusive social functions and guaranteed to have no emotional complications.

Constant activities hid me from loneliness. With no one close, or intimate. Only Mary. We had a connection, despite remaining aloof to her affections. Although as much as we got on, I could never imagine looking into her eyes and telling her of my passion for murder. Deep down, I longed for a way to break free from myself. From the pain, from the cruelty. From the voice. Surely a good woman could help me? A woman who loved me. But how could anyone ever love me? Entrenched urges to commit homicide could not be sated by domestic passivity, no matter how comforting, or encompassing. Not ever. Loneliness drove my decision to use an alias.

Instinct, or ignorance. One of these beguiled and convinced me affection could be found even with such an artificial personality. An identity apart from every other aspect of my real life. Keeping things at a reasonable distance, but still attaining the warmth I craved.

This turbulent concoction of factors combined. Coercing me to develop the alias Dan Turner into a full-blown alter-ego. A fictional character of my own making, created in order to find some kind of normal relationship with Val. Perhaps the culture of nicknames or "Handles" used by the CB community had got a hold of my imagination. Or perchance my loneliness had become so desperate I'd try anything to feel some form of intimacy.

"Sam, the representatives from Southern Minerals Conglomerate are requesting your presence at their board meeting on the eighteenth", Mary said to me over the crackling hotel telephone. My room at the Imperial in Grantham being the only one with its own private connection. The rest of the guests had to go down to the lobby. The telephone being an ancient looking object. A bulky old nineteen-forties thing, made of chunky Bakelite. Heavier and more solid than the modern plastic versions. Hefting the receiver, you could bash a man's face in with it. I grabbed the chord in both hands, it felt thick and resilient between my fingers. Stout enough to strangle someone.

'Now there's a thought. Two, actually.'
'Can't you ever stop?'
'Do you realise how ridiculous that question is? Do you think you could ever stop?'
'For what? There will always be someone who deserves to die.'
'For your own salvation, perhaps.'
'It's far too late for that.'
'But is it?'

Mary knew I'd only agree to certain meetings with particular associates. Keeping me well-informed with plenty of notice and reminders. This call went against these parameters. "Is it important?" I asked, irritated by the interruption.

"Important enough. You are on their board of directors."

"I know, I know. But didn't I go last year?"

"That was three years ago. You're supposed to go every year. We've run out of viable excuses." Mary spoke in a dry, business-like manner. Then her voice mellowed, taking on the personal touch usually reserved for our private intimacies. "You have nothing else booked for over a month afterwards Sam, can't you come down to London? I'd love to spend an evening with you, if you have the time." Her velvet tones and honey voice melted through the cranky old receiver, pouring like molten gold to thaw my frozen, lonely heart.

"How could I resist an offer like that? What day did you say again?" An impulsive burst of enthusiasm propelling the words from my mouth with plain joy ringing in their tones. The thought of being able to relax with Mary and forget about my darker mentality for a few days drew me with a powerful magnetism.

"I didn't. I said the date. The eighteenth. It's a Thursday. You can take me out afterwards and still get back to whatever you're doing up there in Lincolnshire by the weekend", she answered, allowing a little friendly impertinence to shine through. As a reminder to how well she knew my business. Better than I did myself. But then, I had my secret work to concentrate on.

"You know Mary, you'll make some lucky fella a good wife someday."

"Is that right? Not had many offers come my way so far, Sam."

"Good. I'd hate to lose you. I couldn't do any of this, this voluntary work I do if it weren't for you Mary. Being able to trust you with my business interests is a God-send. I hope you realise that."

"Aww, you are sweet Sam, thank you. But you don't have to worry, I have no intentions of going anywhere. I know where I'm needed."

"And appreciated!" I blurted; tone full of integrity. Mary knew I meant every word.

"Shall I tell the lady from Southern Minerals you'll be there this year then?"

"Yes, do that. I'll be there."

"Next week then."

"Next week."

Mary and I kept in touch by post as well as telephone. With the telegram service a last resort. Calling her my secretary amused both of us, being such an obvious understatement. Committing her life to keeping my ship afloat. Her constant dedication and diligence enabled me to commit time to my tasks. I paid her very well for her services. Brought her a solid gold pension plan, a handsome nest-egg and the house in Chelsea as a retainer. Mary should have been my wife, but I craved murder. There could be no other way the two could exist in my life together.

CLOSET CASE

B rian Vickerstaff lived close to the diminutive ancient city of Lincoln. In a hamlet nestled among the picturesque Lincolnshire Wolds. I'd decided to stay in the county to be close to the coast during the summer months.

Archives in Lincoln's main library brought Brian to my attention. Pre-eminent among a plethora of ne'er-do-wells and degenerates to be found there. A smirking former policeman. A bully who drove a sick man to suicide. An act responsible for the passing of the same man's elderly mother, who dropped down dead upon hearing the news of her son's untimely passing. This left her husband alone, frail and grieving. Grief which took him to the grave within months of his son's suicide. The whole family wiped out within the year.

Brian loved to tell people of his former career. Didn't dwell on why he'd had to leave the force though. On paper of course he had medical issues. A heart problem meaning he couldn't work in a stressful environment. The reality of it told a different story. Clumsy corruption had caught him out. Superiors brushed it under the table to avoid a full public inquiry, but on a local level, people knew the truth.

Brian would have been my next Target. Weeks into the surveillance period however, my plan in place, all at once, everything changed. Martin Alsop walked in and altered my whole perception of the situation. Brian liked to frequent a pub on a crossroads a few miles South of Lincoln on the A15. I would sit in the restaurant side, eating lunch. Recognising Martin's face as Brian stood to greet him. Yet Martin's name eluded me until later, when alone in the hotel room. From my time in Durham, once those news reports had come back to me. Then a plan to kill the pair of them, together, began taking root in my savage imagination.

'Kill two birds with one stone.'
'Twice the risk.'
'Twice the pleasure. You know it's true.'
'Correct. I can hardly wait.'
'You will revel in it.'

Like a mantra, the thought encompassed and intrigued my mind. Day and night. Intense surveillance then provided the factor necessary to make my dream a reality. Discovering Brian and Martin met up and spent whole days together. Somewhere rural. Finding out where they went and for what purpose, on these, most often weekend days, soon became the key to this Hit.

Slaying them both in separate incidents on the same night would have involved less risk. But the sheer challenge of the idea drew me on and on. Deeper into the fantasy of it. Visualising murdering the pair of degenerates and leaving their corpses side by side in a grim parody of their friendship evoked vitriolic sadism to arise in my bosom.

Getting to them whilst alone together. How to solve this problem? Predicting their movements with enough accuracy for them both to be where expected, when expected, proved to be a conundrum worth the effort of solving.

Birds of a Feather

Martin Alsop. The Yorkshire Set's finest, who got away with burying his housemaid. Cold-hearted, self-centred. Born wealthy. A man whose wife's trauma showed in her eyes, despite the big hair, fine jewellery and furs. Martin struggled to get along with women. Lacking the ability to engage with them or form relationships of any depth. His poor wife, a mere trophy. A former beauty queen. Childless, through no fault of her own. Young, naïve and ignorant of her husband's contempt. At least to begin with.

Martin had desired a heritage. One carrying his name, to last long into the generations of his descendants. A business empire of some kind. However, lacking heirs, he'd seethed with frustrated, covert rage. Allowing blame and spite to fester in his heart. Their marriage became a social shell, absent of any bond, intimacy or companionship. Martin went on to take out his frustrations on the live-in house maids.

All this according to the prosecution at his hearing in York. No-one else knows the truth of what happened except Martin and those poor young women. A sexual motive had rated high on the prosecution's list. My gut feeling resonated with this theory. The behaviours and emotions he displayed whilst under my own observations also testified to it.

<hr />

Weeks of concerted observation produced consistent results. To the point where I knew when to expect the nefarious pair of miscreants to meet up. Always at the same large, traveller's-rest type country pub, The Griffin, out on the A15 in Lincolnshire. One particular weekend, whilst monitoring Brian, the two of them met on the pub's car-park at eight o'clock on the Saturday morning. Hours prior to opening time. Brian jumped in Martin's Range Rover and they sped off, heading North. I managed to keep in touch with them, driving the Jaguar XJ6 I'd bought for the Hit on Mark Walpole. Staying behind far enough not to arouse suspicion. Heavy clouds from the coast closed in and a rain spall hit as we crossed the Humber bridge. Boxed-in between a slow horse-trailer and an eighteen-wheeled wagon, they disappeared from view into the spray. Once clear, the Range-Rover had gone. They'd taken an exit whilst out of my line of vision.

⟫◆⟪

A fortnight later, they met up again. Same routine, although on this occasion I lost touch with them in Ripley. Traffic got between us and a change of lights put them too far ahead. They turned off onto a steep, wending B-road. By the time I got to the same road they were gone, up, or down one of two turn-offs. Left or right, how could I tell? Adventuring along these took me twisting around endless blind-bends, further and deeper into the dale. To no avail.

'Your diligence is impressive.'

'Finding out where these two go together is my divine duty.'

'You could have been a detective.'

'They deserve it. I want to kill them together, as one.'

'To indulge your bloodlust further?'

'Merely being efficient.'

'You think so?'

On the next occasion, I anticipated their journey. Three weekends passed before they met up again, same time of day. As always, in fine weather. By now early September had brought significant rainfall, albeit overnight, in general. The days being full of blue skies and fluffy, innocent clouds. That particular weekend stayed fine and bright. Hence their getting together on the Saturday.

Same time, same place. Except in this instance, I got past them and raced ahead. Well ahead. Putting miles between us. Creating time to park out of sight in a hidden spot with a clear view of the approach. Sure enough, within an hour, Martin's white Range Rover came along. Watching from a half mile away, sat against a large Walnut tree. Peering through an outstanding pair of Bar & Stroud civilian binoculars, anticipating their next move. The Bar & Stroud's were intended for Ornithological use, primarily. An inspiration picked up from The Crook, Phil Guy. Then Martin's Range-Rover all at once slowed to make a turn, but without a junction in sight.

No wonder I'd lost track of them the previous occasion. Martin turned between the large hedgerows through an open gate, hidden from the lane in a field of rough grass, bracken and sedges. Peering through the first-rate binoculars, I scanned the environment. Martin had parked up close to a sprawling Holly shrub, both men were out and he opened the back. Within, two shelves divided the luggage space top to bottom. From these Brian withdrew two large model aircraft, their controllers and other associated kit. At that moment for the first time their shared activity revealed itself in full. The fiendish friends then set about starting the engines and testing the controllers. Those miniature motors made a terrific high-pitched racket. Listening to them buzzing, they reminded me of wasps and mosquitoes. The sound irritated. Hurting my ears. Clattering all over the peaceful English setting.

'Of course.'

'Of course, what?'

'You know this is perfect?'

'Really?'

'Killing them here will be a pleasure.'

'Not today though. I'm not prepared.'

'No. Anticipation shall heighten the enjoyment.'

'I hope so.'

'This shall prove to be a labour of love.'

'Yes. Love of God.'

'You cannot pretend you needed any encouragement.'

'Being the Wrath of God on Earth is all the encouragement I need.'

'*Well then. Go to your work.*'

'My Duty.'

'*You really intend to kill both men together?*'

'I'll leave them dead on the cold ground.'

'*Then find a way to kill these two birds with one stone. Do it.*'

STONE COLD

Late September, during a whole week of sunshine, the familiar signs became apparent. Recorded indicators confirmed Brian and Martin were preparing for a drive to Yorkshire with their expensive model aircraft the approaching weekend. Meanwhile, the Jaguar concerned me, having been up and down those country roads too many times. I'd already decided to make an arrangement with Val. The Jag needed to be ditched as soon as this Hit had been executed.

Val and I came to an arrangement. One which would prove extra lucrative for her, due to my promise to pay twice her usual asking price in return for meeting specific requirements. To meet up somewhere innocuous and take the car to her place, on the evening of the Hit. Of course, Val knew nothing of my intended murders, but I had to allude to the Jag being used for something dubious. Therefore, my presence would be required to ensure of the car's complete destruction. Her trust and diligence were further gained by posting a substantial cheque to a P.O. Box address Val supplied as a deposit. All my pieces were in place. Next time Brian and Martin flew their expensive model planes, would be the day of their doom.

Fog covered the Yorkshire moors on the morning of the Hit. I awaited the Targets there, having driven up at five am. It occurred to me they might not show up due to the weather. Placing myself out of sight beneath a hedgerow, wrapped in woollens and waterproofs, I settled down and focused on preventing stiffness from developing in my joints. Time passed very slow laying there. Worry about them not showing kept bubbling into my thoughts. However, I flexed and stretched my limbs to keep the circulation flowing and my mind occupied on the task. Whilst waiting, visualising striking the pair down side by side, brought blood pulsing through my ears with demonic intensity.

'To kill two birds with one stone...'

The phrase, as applied to my intentions, kept me occupied with cruel designs. Bloodlust incarnated into a savage plan of brutal execution. This devilish pair had to be disposed of at speed, by complete and utter surprise. Shooting them down with a hunting bow, like docile, grazing cattle as they stared skyward, enthralled in their activity, had occurred to me. But no. Each man had to know they were being killed together. I wanted them to die wondering why.

'Kill two birds with one stone...' Drove me into unleashing the callousness inside to full effect. The setting seemed too perfect not to.

My early concerns turned out to be unfounded. The fog lifted mid-morning, the sunshine grew hot and a few minutes prior to Midday sounds of Martin's Range Rover roared up the hillside. He pulled into the field, shattering the passive noises of distant sheep, buzzing insects and moorland wildfowl, which had soothed my ears during the preceding laconic hours. Rolling over with care to prop my head and watch them set up, my heart rate increased. Their routine involved flying the model aircraft for some time, after initial checks were done. The pair of them would end up stood staring skyward, radio-controller in hands, engrossed in performing stunts with their expensive toys.

Estimating forty minutes would have to pass prior to making a move, I waited, watching with intent. They each did a few short preliminary flights, checking the controls, the batteries and engines, before committing to a long session of constant flight. This latter being preceded by Brian opening a flask of coffee and the pair of them enjoying a cigarette each along with their drinks. Twenty minutes into the long flight, both men stood almost drooling in concentration. Each wearing silver-framed, Aviator mirror-sunglasses. Those model airplanes weren't so big once up in the sky and could be difficult to see with the glare of the sun in your eyes. I remember feeling a level of appreciation for the focus it took to control the things from the ground. Somehow, it helped me do away with Brian and Martin in the cruel and ferocious manner I'd chosen.

'*Get up and kill them.*'
'Watch me.'

Pushing up from the ground I climbed to my feet, weapon in hand. Brian and Martin had their backs to me. Ahead of them the ground dropped away into the valley, they preferred to fly the planes there, avoiding having to look upwards at acute angles so much. It must have been the reason they chose the place to practise their hobby. The land belonged to Martin; I believe. Or a close friend of his. A local landowner he knew through his Masonic connections.

I had to act fast. The ariels of the radio-controllers stuck out around four feet, meaning Brian and Martin kept a few yards apart whilst flying their planes. Approaching them became an unanticipated issue. A section of the field between myself and the Targets held a substantial amount of Sedge-grass, containing water deeper than it appeared. Bumpy, bog-like and a difficult hindrance. This detail of the terrain had escaped my notice up to that moment.

Cursing in whispers. Trudging across bouncy clumps of deep grass between soggy hollows of cold water. Knowing I had to improvise to make the double-kill work. Walking around the boggy piece of ground didn't even enter my head. If either man saw me and landed his plane before I could instigate my move - game over. Maintaining the surprise factor, allowing them to stay focused on flying, even if they did sense me approaching, were vital to the Hit.

Heading in a direct line, I got close to them quick enough. But keeping an eye on either man whilst crossing the boggy piece of ground proved impossible. Brian noticed my struggling form in the corner of his eye. Half-glancing over his shoulder, he asked;

"Who's that?" Brian's words followed by Martin's in an instant; -

"That you Trevor?", he called, eyes on the model plane, buzzing away high above, to his left. His blind side, from my point of view. These few words cost the men vital time to react. Their casual queries and attitude to my approach allowed me to cross those last few, crucial yards.

"No, but he sends his regards", I lied, to keep them focused on their hobby. It worked. My lie took me within reach of Brian. Exaggerating the last two strides, I threw my right arm around in an arc as though bowling at the Oval for England. Centrifugal force combining with momentum accelerated the fling of my hand. In it I held a large cobble, fished from a streambed at the bottom of the valley early on that bloody morning.

Weighing about five pounds, the smooth, ovoid stone accelerated into Brian's right cheek. Crack! Stone smashed bone. He fell with a guttural noise to the ground. His model aeroplane made an unusual, drastic blare of noise, as the engine revs screamed to full and the thing went out of control. Before it had crashed into the muddy ground, I'd already crossed the space between the two men.

Martin had no chance. Caught mid-turn. Reacting to the sound and motion of my assault on Brian, he met the concentrated force of my next blow in the centre of his face. Nose and mandible were crushed. Blood and mucus caused me to lose grip on the stone and he fell to the ground twitching with the cobble embedded in his face. He didn't twitch for long, as I pressed my foot onto the stone until he stopped clawing and scratching at my boot. Pulling the cobble out of Martin's face turned into a frenzy of rage and revulsion as slime, blood and nastiness squelching between my fingers made the task disgusting. Meanwhile, Brian had struggled to his knees and Martin's expensive model aircraft had also crashed, buzzing and whining into the soft moorland.

The large cobble stuck to my hands due to all the gore smeared across it. Booting Brian back down, it soon crushed his skull with ease. The first two blows stopped him struggling. Then, horrible gurgling noises, in addition to Martin's mess on my fingers, disgusted me so much I smashed the stone again and again onto Brian's bald head in a frenzy driven by abhorrence and revulsion.

Misdirected hate and rage ignited dynamite repugnance. In an explosion of savagery both exhilarating and shocking. The harder I struck Brian's ruined head, the more brains, slime, and gore spurted into my face. The more I roared in uncontrolled raging violence, the more of his filthy remains spewed into my gaping mouth. The more this happened, the harder I struck him. Until nothing remained worth hitting.

———◆———

Long minutes spent sat astride Brian's yielding body in smouldering triumph. Grabbed handfuls of grass, wiped the cobble, then dropped the cold stone with a resigned thump beside the warm corpse. I used my Arran jumper to clean the worst of the sticky mess from my head and face before pulling a woollen hat from a coat pocket and covering my tacky hair.

A murder of crows cawed and clacked overhead. Disturbed by the wild, crashing model aircraft and the abrupt ferocity on the quiet, secluded field. Staring down at the mess, it occurred to me the crows might take their frustrations out on the silent corpses once I'd left the grisly scene. Taking in the image of Brian's death one last time, I sniffed at the cold air. Knowing grim satisfaction. Retribution Personified. Feeling magnificent, having made the World a better place. I turned and walked away, leaving Martin faceless and Brian with his teeth embedded in the soft Yorkshire turf.

STAR-CROSSED

Torrential rain and thunderstorms marred the journey South. Causing slight delays due to flooding throughout Lincolnshire. However, Val would be well aware of this. Windscreen wipers going full-pelt in the Monsoon-like downpour, I pulled the Jaguar into a quiet road, half a mile from the Transit van's location, stashed there the evening prior. After securing the car and walking through the less savage but equally wet rain over to the van, the engine took three wheezing attempts at turning over before sputtering bad-tempered into life. Allowing the motor to warm up and getting as dry as possible, I switched the CB on to contact Val, as arranged. Within a few minutes she replied and provided directions. After moving the van to another spot close by, and returning to the XJ6, I drove to the rendezvous Val had just given me.

We met for the second time in a car-park on a small industrial area by the A10 in Norfolk. Val stepped from her 1970 White Rover P6, beckoning me over as she did. Attraction crackled between us. Something told me we would end up making trouble together. An urge to be involved with Val commenced from then on. The fact we were acquainted under my alias helped. Allowing me freedom to mould the character to appeal to her. We didn't talk much in the car park. A mere acknowledgement, the exchange of cash, then Val said;

"Follow me close Dan, I drive fast."

She did. Thrashing the Rover as if chased by the police. Struggling to stay on the road, never mind keep up, had my eyes out on stalks. With relief, after thirty minutes of this whacky racing, my wide eyes picked out an indicator blinking out in the gloom.

We turned right into a long, gated driveway. The first several hundred yards of which had a smooth tarmac surface, with open fields on either side. Then we went over a hump-back bridge and around a small bend which seemed to exist just to avoid a massive and ancient Black Elm. Beyond that point the drive became a mere gravel track between hedgerows of Hawthorn and Lonicera, well-worn and full of ruts and small pot holes. Between tall shrubs we bumped and bounced for another quarter mile before the Rover swung into an opening and parked up. Val sprang out of the car but left it running, radio still playing the latest disco tunes. Dark shrouded the area, my eyes still adjusting from the relative brightness of the headlights. Before my sight revealed where we stood, Val spoke.

"Don't worry, we won't be here long. Have you got everything you need out of it?

"Yes," I nodded, patting myself down. "All here."

"You sure? Wouldn't want to find someone taking a long nap in the back, if you know what I mean, eh?" Val's speech reminded me of the style of a much older woman, yet the tones of her voice carried an unmistakeable magnetism. In the same moment our eyes met. An irrepressible chuckle loosened the tension between us and we shared a smile.

"Yep, she's all clear."

"She, eh?"

"Of course." I answered with a wink. "Aren't they all?"

"I suppose, whatever pleases you. I know how men feel about their cars Dan, believe me."

"I meant all things men build are called she. All vehicles that is."

"Like a ship you mean? A boat?"

"That's it, or even an aeroplane. I give my cars a woman's name."

"Oh yeah?" Val smiled and lit a John Players cigarette, offering me one before shaking my hand with affected politeness. "Very sweet, I like you mister, like you already. You're a good 'un aren't ya?" She gestured with a thumb towards my car. "So, what do you call this one then?"

"She is called Janey. Janey the Jag", I smiled.

"Well, can I have the keys to Janey the Jag then please, Danny the man?" She exaggerated the last words with an affected accent.

"Why not?" Replying whilst pulling said keys from my jacket pocket and handing them to her.

"No other keys on here you need?" She asked, looking at the large, leather Jaguar keyring with a frown.

"No. They're just some old keys on there that are no use to me. She's all yours now." Val threw the keys into a pocket and grinned.

"Good. Now Dan, you go and get in my car. Don't mind Olly, she won't bite, but don't let her climb all over you or you'll never get her off."

"Olly?"

"My little bow-wow, she's friendly though, too friendly."

"Will you be long?" I asked, unsure of the prospect of being with a strange, over-sociable dog.

"Five minutes. Just need to put Janey to bed for you." She answered through the driver's window then drove into the gloom. The headlights of the Jag revealed a short drive ahead of her through another gate into a concrete compound hidden behind a row of tall Poplar trees. I stepped into her car and had to fuss the dog, a lively, if diminutive Jack Russell Terrier bitch, until Val returned. Spotlights came on behind the trees and large machinery whirred into action as the crusher came to life. Val operated a grabber to lift the car. The noise level increased as engines worked hard and the car protested being compressed.

"In the back", Val commanded Olly, opening the driver's door and getting in, before swinging the car out of the compound and back down the bumpy lane.

"Here's the rest of the money we agreed, plus an extra fifty quid for your trouble." Placing the cash bundle on her lap. We had planned for Val to drop me off at Lincoln. Slender, red-nailed fingers took the money and deposited it out of sight with a mesmerising degree of dexterity and economy of motion.

"No need, but thanks anyway." Val's smooth tones were clement to my ears. I liked her voice more and more each time she spoke.

"You're welcome, for the inconvenience, the fuel, you know."

"It's no bother Dan, I like a run over to Lincoln now and then, It's a nice drive. Besides I still own a couple of boats in one of the marinas over there."

"Canal boats?" The question seemed stupid. Val answered without sarcasm or judgement though.

"Yeah, narra'- boats. I rent 'em out. You ever been on a narra'-boat?" Her accent made me smile.

Narrowboats. Left over from an erstwhile era. Now either laying in disrepair around the country or refurbished and dwelled in, like watery caravans. With a few working boats thrown in. Moored up semi-permanently in marinas, they produced a unique kind of transient existence in the backwaters of England and Wales.

"Actually yes. In my youth. The village youth club I belonged to; they took some of us on a short holiday in one."

"Oh yeah, sounds like fun. D'ya remember whereabouts?"

"Think we were somewhere between Nottingham and Derby, if my memory serves me well."

"Hmm, could've been the Trent n' Mersey canal, depending how good your memory is" Val winked at me.

The journey to Lincoln in Val's Rover went on in the same congenial manner. Aided by the fact Val drove slower. Plus, our flirting became less and less subtle. Each of us needing to let the other know our desire.

This flirtatiousness dwindled as we drew closer to the destination. Superseded by a tinge of discomfiture. The intimacy of the enclosed space restricting proper understanding. Until a shared smile, once Val could take her eyes from the road and look at me for a few seconds, relaxed our mutual doubts a few minutes before she dropped me off. Then when she did, Val made sure I'd gotten the message.

"Be sure to throw me a line, breaker one-nine." Her alluring voice purred, winking slow and seductive, eyes locked on mine.

"Copy that, kitty-cat." I ad-libbed, surprising myself by affecting a corny Yank drawl, then kissing the tips of my index and middle finger and blowing her a kiss, before turning and striding towards the station as though I were James Dean.

STRICTLY BUSINESS

Following this encounter with Val, I became torn. Between myself and my alias. Between logic and adventure, the head and the heart. Time and again, I'd go out driving around South Lincolnshire, using the CB radio rigged up in the Transit to try and catch Val on the airwaves. Albeit maintaining focus through all the irrelevant CB chatter required immense patience.

A handful of times over a month, 'Vienna Rose' piped up. The familiar tones springing through the static as she engaged in general CB banter and exchange of traffic information. Hearing her voice thrilled me. We'd exchange words of greeting, then choose a channel to speak on. Just chatter, innocuous stuff. Our on-air flirting only served to highlight the serious attraction we had for each other. Meanwhile however, back in my real life, business consultations had to be rearranged, golf meets cancelled and sound investment opportunities were missed.

Because of this, Mary had to perform wonders on my behalf. Claiming to some parties I'd travelled overseas to attend a family funeral; others were told I'd had to book time at a retreat due to stress. We'd used similar excuses and strategies before. Albeit not with more than one firm at a time and never without Mary knowing the exact reason behind my late cancellations.

I sensed Mary's curiosity prick up. A certain tone to her innocent-sounding questions caught my ear. Like a bloodhound, she never lost a scent. I knew that curiosity of hers would lead her to the truth, or at least the truth of a woman being involved in my life in some significant way.

Did Mary love me? I often wondered about it. She never alluded to do so. Not in words, but in action...indeed. Her fretting endured me to her, but I thought of it as merely her need to take care of the golden goose. Over time though, I came to realise such thoughts only reflected my own cynicism. Experience went on to teach me her dedication and commitment were neither manufactured or contrived in any way.

However, back then I couldn't see it. Not until hearing the tone of jealousy in Mary's voice over the 'phone. Explaining to her once more how I'd be staying up in the Midlands. Missing more meetings and social events. Mary's concerns came from the fact that my attendance at these meetings and events had been arranged with great care.

Mary knew the routine. Months of me living away in the provinces, with meetings and appointments kept at a minimum and with at least a weeks' notice, excepting special cases. Then beyond a certain date I'd be free for engagements and soon back in London.

Except this time around things had changed. After Mark Walpole, my fascination for CB radio meant I'd maintained the distance. Cancelled appointments, rescheduled meetings. Mary couldn't help being curious.

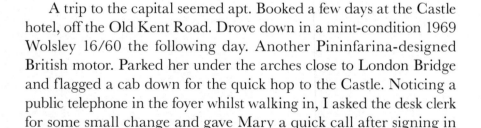

A trip to the capital seemed apt. Booked a few days at the Castle hotel, off the Old Kent Road. Drove down in a mint-condition 1969 Wolsley 16/60 the following day. Another Pininfarina-designed British motor. Parked her under the arches close to London Bridge and flagged a cab down for the quick hop to the Castle. Noticing a public telephone in the foyer whilst walking in, I asked the desk clerk for some small change and gave Mary a quick call after signing in as Mr and Mrs Prenton. After three rings she answered. "Busy?" I enquired, acting nonchalant.

"Sam! Where are you?" She replied, instantly recognising my voice, sharp as ever.

"London. Old Kent Road. Waiting for you."

"You could have told me you were coming back down Sam!" Her reprimanding tone reaching right through the earpiece. "You know I like to look good for you."

"All right, all right Mary, nothing to worry about. Take your time, I've only just arrived. Still need to get my bags up to the room and unpack. Then I'll order a sandwich and some booze from room service and get in the bath. You're all booked in as my wife, there's a key waiting for you at the desk. Come straight up."

"You will never cease to surprise me, Sam Daniels."

"Truer words may never be spoken Mary, believe me."

<hr>

She arrived whilst I enjoyed the large, free-standing, cast-iron bath. A characteristic, Edwardian-Period beauty, in immaculate condition. Almost deep enough to dive into.

True to form, Mary had dressed for the occasion and looked fantastic. Beautiful, curvy, alluring and petite as ever. I got out the bath as she prepared drinks and put on the flip-side of the L.P. record I'd been listening to whilst in there. One of Herbie Hancock's albums of the time.

With rum and cola fuelling my ardour I ravished Mary in the lounge, the kitchen and, just to be civilised, the bedroom. Albeit, my passion became so aroused, some of the carnal acts we delighted in were not those prescribed by the Church.

We spent three days together at the hotel. In which time we worked on rebuilding the structure of my business arrangements. I made up a story about needing to spend more time away from London, refraining from details. Only that I'd be based in the East Midlands. She knew it somehow involved a woman. Despite Mary doing all she could to disguise her knowledge, it declared itself loud and clear. A subtle level of awkwardness hung between us. Most of the time we shared a strong sense of intimacy but when I spoke of my reasons for these changes, my necessary lies hurt both our ears. Then we'd avoid the issue, yet an undercurrent had been set.

The realisation Mary loved me came during this phase. Those particular few days we spent together spoke volumes. However, the fact Mary had already deduced that I was also in love with her failed to penetrate my ken. Moreover, she understood my denial. Unable to admit it even to myself.

Selfishness overrode my senses. For I wanted her to love all of me. Yet how could a man ever tell a woman he commits such acts of violence? Dark desires and brutal fantasies dreamed, planned and executed into terrible reality? Could a woman feel safe around a cold-blooded murderer? Could she also justify his actions, within her own conscience? I could not imagine Mary's considerations would possess the depths of savagery my own held. What woman could live with such things? Yet, my need to find a normal existence could no longer be denied.

⬗◆⬖

The preoccupation to meet Val consumed my thoughts. Creating viable reasons to do so, without affecting her reservations being most pertinent. Also, the matter of perfecting being Dan Turner. Beforehand, signing into a hotel under an assumed name for a few days had never been a problem. In my experience, with plenty of hard cash on show, no desk clerk ever asks too many questions.

Yet in this case, my intention carried greater risk than the mere deception of strangers. Involving pretending to be a person who did not exist, on numerous, subsequent occasions. To involve myself with a woman I would need to lie to again and again, in order to maintain the charade. All for pure indulgence. A prodigious and perpetual homesickness burned in my heart. Pushing this agenda. Propelling me towards an unforeseeable calamity of my own making. An obligatory and disastrous collision of fates.

⬗◆⬖

Cars were part of Val's business. The Wolsley came in handy as an excuse to book her services once more. However, storage being the choice, as that particular car held an emotional attachment for me. Val must have guessed my intentions as she made sure we had plenty of time alone together. We went out to a pub in the nearest village and the night went well. Val invited me to stay over and she once again took me to Lincoln the following morning.

Within a few weeks we repeated the process. Crushing the vehicle, this time a Luton van I'd picked up at auction in Cambridge a week prior. Giving Val the impression the van had been used in some serious crime down in London and needed disposing of. Familiarity with the Old Smoke helped. Implying my role involved bringing vehicles used by professional criminals based in the capital, up to Norfolk, well away from any Metropolitan Police feelers.

Before long, a routine developed. I'd make an arrangement to meet with Val on a Friday evening. We'd meet up, spend a few minutes talking in her car. She would lead me back to her place. My vehicle would be disposed of, I'd pay her above her asking price each time for the service. Once business had been sorted, Val would drive us out to eat somewhere cosy, before enjoying a few drinks in a country pub. Later on, we'd make our way back to her place, get merry and play records, enjoying great nights together.

Once alone, we could never keep our hands off each other. But Val remained unneedy, independent. As if she didn't require me at all. She didn't. Yet, she encouraged my company. It felt good to be Dan. Using a false name and identity to find a little nirvana in a close companionship did not seem too indulgent. Reasoning no-one would be harmed.

Business interests compelled me to reside in Nottingham for several weary, wintery months. This central location provided easy access to London and Birmingham by train for a few important engagements. But it also put me out of range with Val by CB, unless I drove to the Transit van, then over to the Fens. This soon became a dull arrangement with late trains and poor roads. Leading me to purchasing a cottage in a village occupying a convenient location on the triple border of Leicestershire, Lincolnshire and Nottinghamshire. A wealthy village called Bottesford. A rural place, but with excellent communications by road and rail to London.

From then, whenever out in the Transit van using the CB radio, I'd dress and speak as Dan Turner. Prior to this, I'd only dressed Dan's way whenever meeting Val. Now, in preparation for playing the role much more often, I took to pretending to be Dan at every opportunity.

Val had independence. With her yard space and machinery providing a steady, legitimate income. Milk, eggs, cheese and butter came from her own small-holdings. She also kept fine gardens of produce. Containing fruit trees and vegetable patches. With berries, beans and vine-fruits grown in a walled garden or one of three brick-built glasshouses. Nonetheless, my perceptions of Val had a shortcoming. A fatal flaw, as events went on to manifest. For as mentioned, there existed a tough, domineering, troublesome influence in her life. Which I had no discernment of. Not until far too late.

New Year

1 978 brought regular time with Val, somewhat quelling my thirst for companionship and belonging. Yet these occasions were always as Dan. The rest of my days, during the week, being alone with little to do, soon felt very empty. Without the purpose of murder in mind, hours spent in the cottage went by as if time had been slowed down to a tectonic crawl.

During springtime, boredom drove me to set up the large aerial and static CB station there. This brought Val's signal within reach, but I preferred only to listen as Dan had alluded that he lived in Essex. Mobile sets were much noisier and made it obvious to the listener you were on the road.

By this time Val and I were hooking up every weekend. She would cook on Sundays, except when we drove out for a pub lunch. Then a light afternoon tea of cold meat sandwiches and pickles before I'd take my leave. Val didn't question me about money, but after our first few dates she did begin to show a curiosity about my work. Or rather, Dan's. We would speak on the CB for a few minutes here and there during the week, whilst I drove up and down the A1 in the Transit van.

One day Val, speaking as 'Vienna Rose' asked; "So, what are you driving today then?" After we'd chosen a free channel to speak on.

"Driving a furniture van up the A1, from Bedford to Hull"

"Hope you get there, how's the road looking?"

"Ok, making good time. Started out early due to the hold-ups around Peterborough mentioned on the radio."

"Good idea, there's usually trouble there in rush hour."

"Yep. Apart from that, the roads been fine. Little busy, with midweek traffic." The old A1, or Great North Road, built by the Romans, progresses like a main artery up the East side of England. This conduit of communication, connecting London to Edinburgh, is steeped in history and tales of yore. For a fifteen mile or so stretch of it, my mobile CB set could reach Val's home equipment.

"Anyway, what you hauling?" She asked.

"Picking up fine furniture and home furnishings in Hull. A load has come over from Holland, for distribution to retailers down South." Weaving my story to give regular occasions to be close enough to connect with Val on the CB. As Dan, this relationship flourished and life began to show some potential for normality.

However, during the rest of the time, life lost its meaning. No murder to look forward to. No secret planning. No surveillance. Now, as I write this, older and wiser, it's easy to see how I'd denied myself several compulsions in order to play Dan Turner. With catastrophic results. Voyeurism, adrenaline, and bloodlust are a terrible combination of addictions. But spiced further with fixation, sadism and sense of purpose, I was a homicide junkie, through and through. In the middle of a deadly delusion, ignorant to the nightmarish, personalised cold-turkey I'd created for myself.

'Can you really play a role and forget who you are?'

"It's not like that.'

'Isn't it?'

'No. More like putting my secret work on hold for a while.'

'Your secret work? How noble. How long will this last?'

'As long as I deem fit, of course.'

'Ah yes. Of course.'

'Like putting it all into a suitcase. I can open it back up whenever I want.'

'Whenever you want? When will that be?'

'When I'm ready.'

'This will not end well. You do realise that don't you?'

'I know what I'm doing.'

'*No. You do not. You are deluded. This course of action is irresponsible.*'

Officious loneliness impacted actuality each day. Despite the independence, trappings and power. By artificial means, I'd implanted a scenario into my experience which did not belong there. In an attempt to control my homicidal tendencies. Concentrating on perfecting being Dan Turner for the weekends, in replacement of stalking and studying a Target. Weekly business calls with Mary provided the only solace. Many nights I spent alone as Dan, driving on the motorways, speaking over the CB with other drivers. This at least kept me informed.

———◆———

Val loved to talk about CB radio issues. Gardening and fishing were other interests which occupied a lot of her time. Listening to her enthusiasm always pleased me. I also enjoyed watching the shine of light play on her straight, dark hair. Hair so thick. Val didn't wear her hair down, instead tying it back or gathering it in bunches for practicality. She often became animated with passion as she spoke, forgetting herself in her enthusiasm and then the light would dance on her locks. Val's zeal for plants, in particular herbs and edible flowers, never ceased. Studying and reading with great care prior to attempting any form of propagation of any unfamiliar plant.

We enjoyed a wonderful Midsummer weekend together. Attending a local music festival held on a field between two of the numerous canals of the North Fens. July laboriously turned into August. Weekdays passed full of tedium and anticipation for the weekend. Our relationship, such as it was, had become "steady", by the time the bomb dropped.

GRAVE ENCOUNTER

As it often does prior to a crisis, life had become idyllic. Without any pressure on the relationship, no long-term commitments, we were at ease with each other. If Val had not been such a tough cookie, the guilt for my deception might have proven too great. I already felt bad enough. The only taint on the whole affair. Dan wasn't who Val took him for. But only playing Dan made any of it possible. Without the role, we could never have become so well acquainted.

We were in Val's largest glasshouse one bright Sunday morning. This one ran along the outside of the South-facing wall of her kitchen garden. The horticultural structure being a relic from the Victorian occupants of the old Lock-Keepers cottage. Val had fresh courgettes and tomatoes in a basket over her left arm as she picked and sorted through vines about her head. Facing her, with my back to the sliding door as it made its unmistakeable squeal of protest at being opened, I at once saw her eyes widen in surprise. Looking over my shoulder towards the sound, Val's eyes now narrowed, her voice hardening.

"What the bloody hell? I thought you were still in Spain?" She exclaimed to whoever had entered.

"Yeah well, I got bored." The voice, deep and masculine, had the same accent as Val's except with an abrupt tone. I remained still, facing Val as the voice went on; "Nah, need to see old Malc about a dog. Who's this then?" The gruff voice challenged.

"This is Dan. He's a good friend of mine. He's alright Sean."

"Yeah? How long you known my sister then, Dan? That your real name, is it? Dan?" The words, spat out like bad tasting food, came with a challenging sneer in the tone. "You treat her right do ya, Danny boy?"

"Of course he fucking does! I told ya, he's alright. No need to talk to him like that, he's my guest."

"I'll decide if he's alright Val. He's fucking aware of me now, isn't he?"

"But he don't know fuck all Sean! And it's your fault for fuckin' turning up out the fuckin' blue! If you'd sent word you were coming Dan wouldn't be here, would he?"

"That don't matter." The man with the voice for the first time moved into my vision. During the entire exchange I remained still and quiet, letting the sudden, surprising change of situation unveil itself. So, Val has a brother. Thoughts flashed into my mind. A criminal. Back from abroad. Probably wanted. Likely to be prone to violence and considered dangerous. Evidently arrogant and aggressive.

Stale beer and cigarette smoke tainted his breath as he stood in front of me, having to stoop beneath tomato vines and getting tutted at by Val for breaking some of them. Before our eyes even met, somehow, I knew. One day I would kill this man.

The moment felt surreal. It must have been caused by a release of adrenaline. My veins turned to ice. A memory came to me in that instant. Of feeling something similar, on occasions as a young man, scared stiff and hyper-alert in a combat zone. Yet this time a cloak of calm kept my reactions in check. Diamond-hard thoughts crushed facts and logic in a blender within my mind. Assimilating the range of sensations within and without, during this unanticipated confrontational encounter.

"You got a tongue in your head or what? Staying quiet, are we Dan? Hoping I'll go away as quick as I just showed up?" Remaining silent I lifted my chin and held his gaze, though without malice. Sean seemed unnerved and wouldn't hold eye contact. Instead turning towards Val as he went on. "Well, think again. Most of the stuff around here is mine. I just let my sister here use it."

"Might as well be mine! Fucking hell Sean! I have as much right to it as you do!"

"Only once I'm dead Val. Then it's all yours." These words, the first he spoke softly, came as sweet music to my ears.

"Sean, you just signed your own death warrant." I said in my deepest, coarsest voice, wrinkling my brow and affecting a serious expression. Then I broke into a grin and stepped forward like an affable acquaintance, hand outstretched. "Only joking!" I blasted, using sheer bombast to disarm him. But Sean did not wish to be disarmed.

"Fuck off ya sweaty bastard. I'm not shaking your hand. You think that's fucking funny? Are you with the law or what? No fucker knows you." He turned to Val; "No one knows him Val. I've been down to the garage, talking to Revs, he says no-one knows your new boyfriend. He's not one of us. He's not even from round here. He could be anyone Val." Sean's instinctive perception of my subterfuge impressed me. Alerting my senses.

'He could prove to be a challenge. Best not underestimate him.'

'Don't worry, I won't.'

"Well, he ain't got no nasty fucking diseases, that's for sure!" Val yelled, her words resonating off the glass walls.

"Do you fucking well have to Val? Is there really any need to go off like that? You should be ashamed. You never spoke like that in front of dad", Sean chided.

"No. And dad weren't stupid enough to bring the law down on himself was he Sean?" Val retorted with a bellyful of ferocity. "He never had to leave the country on account of being summonsed to court to go to prison neither, did he?" She hissed; eyes wide with anger.

"Well, just who is he then?" The question spat out with venom, ignoring her objections. Val looked over at me before answering her overbearing and obnoxious sibling. Her eyes seeking some understanding, even forgiveness from me, for being spoken about as if I weren't there.

"Dan's a decent bloke Sean. He sought my services. I was referred to him by a trusted contact. He paid me well, in advance for an easy job. I knew he must be kosher for us because he obviously needed to cover his own tracks. Now, I don't know what he had to cover up, don't know what he has to hide from the law Sean, we've never spoke of it. That's business. This is pleasure. They don't mix. You know how much I trust my gut and I felt from the start that Dan here has blood on his hands. Not innocent blood though. Whatever he's done to others, I knew he wouldn't harm me and he hasn't. Now you've embarrassed us by pushing me into saying things out loud I'd rather not have."

"Alright, alright. Fuck it I'll leave you two alone then", Sean spluttered. Then muttering as he turned around; "Pair of fucking weirdos." Before asserting as he strode towards the door; - "Don't worry, I won't be far away Val, I'll be close by. And I'm telling you this," he turned, pointing, "He don't scare me, anyone can pull a fucking trigger." Pointing, yet not looking at me. Despite playing the alias, pretending to be Dan Turner, a certain air of menace still surrounded me. Then Sean left, slamming the sliding doors together as he went.

Val broke open a pack of John Players, offering me one as she picked up a Ronson, using it to light her own. Her hand shook a little as she did so, adrenaline coursing through her veins. Not feeling the awkwardness Val imagined, I let my fingers stroke the back of her hand as I took the lighter from her. Her shoulders rose as she took a long draw on the cigarette, falling again faster as she exhaled smoke with obvious agitation.

"Sorry about him. He's an idiot."

"No worries, no accounting for family." I winked at her. Taking time to pull on my own cigarette before blowing the smoke upwards, I gave her a look of comradeship; "My family are a little weird themselves. I know what families are like. No need to apologise."

"No Dan, there is. Sean's trying to throw some weight around because he knows he fucked up in the first place. Otherwise, he'd have been here all along. You would have already met, under better circumstances." She pulled again on the John Player before continuing. "You would have done if Sean was anything like our dad, anyway."

"You miss your father, don't you?" This query designed to steer the conversation away from my homicidal feelings towards her brother.

"God yes. He held everything together. It's only out of the respect dad built up around these parts that I get treated so well and left alone. But of course, big brother Sean thinks it's out of fear, of him."

"How long since you lost your dad?"

"Four years. I haven't seen Sean since March last year. He had to leave the country. At first, he went to Spain over his own stupid mouth, bragging about a big robbery he'd been part of."

"So, the police are after him?"

"Police, CID, Interpol. You name it. They're all after him."

"He's lucky to stay out of their hands then. No wonder he's tetchy with me. I'm a stranger to him."

"I wouldn't say he's lucky." Val observed, with a cool, discarding flick of the used cigarette.

⮞◆⮜

Thus went my first encounter with Sean Frobisher. Val went on to tell me about his life and where she felt he'd gone really off-course. A sorry tale of indulgence, ego and excess. As unoriginal as the man himself. It came as no surprise to hear Val describe her brother as; - *'Someone who makes enemies easily'*. Yet it seemed he had a certain amount of control over her. He did have co-ownership of the property. With no other siblings nor children between them, either one would inherit the rest from the other. This fact, once revealed, finalised my decision to kill Sean.

Albeit this did vex me. As Dan Turner, the thought of dispatching my lover's imperious brother should not have crossed my mind. Looking back now, it's easy to see the truth. Murderous urges controlled my every move. No matter what I tried to do to deny them. Attempting to subdue these primal longings with this parlour performance of pretence only proved to be calamitous.

ON THE SCENT

From then on, when not speaking to Val, I ceased playing Dan at all. In any way. Homicidal thoughts demanded attention. Vindictive traits within now awoken, longed to rescind Val's blatant sibling. Yet avoiding the urge to kill had been my intention all along. The precise motivation behind developing the Dan Turner alias. Vast reservoirs of suppressed violence and frustrated savagery took the opportunity to hijack my mind.

> *'Good, isn't it?'*
> **'Here we go again.'**
> *'Come on! You know you've missed it.'*
> **'Have I?'**
> *'You love it. This is what you do best.'*
> **'Perhaps.'**
> *'It's what gives you most pleasure.'*
> **'No. Most satisfaction. And purpose.'**
> *'Are you sure?'*

Sean had to be brought somehow within my murderous grasp. I began scheming to devise a method of making this desire come to pass. However, Mary needed me in London the following week for a crucial trade conference. This went better than expected, snapping me back into business mode, and the lurking fiend within slunk back down into the stygian depths of my psyche.

> *'Not for long though.'*
> **'No. Not long at all.'**

Before returning to the East Midlands, I contacted Val and suggested we go out. My alias Dan could not have affluence to my

120

extent. Not with any level of integrity. Too much talk of wealth or influence would raise Val's suspicions. But Dan could come across as lucky and well-informed enough to turn up with a wad of cash once in a while. This Val found intriguing, presuming he'd earned it through gambling, or nefarious activities.

⟫◦⟪

We met up on a sunny day in Boston, Lincolnshire. Rain had washed the streets all night and steam rose from drying tarmac as sunlight twinkled out between the shadows. I'd driven up in a green, 1972 Humber Sceptre, which seemed an appropriate car for Dan to choose as his own. Val hopped down from the cab of her alternate ride – a white 1967 Ford pick-up truck, avoiding the puddles in calf-length boots before reaching for the passenger door of the Humber, as I leaned over to click it open for her.

We took a drive over to Lincoln, and ate at a pleasant Italian restaurant with a lively atmosphere. Not too expensive, but classy enough for Val to feel comfortable. It was an older place, tarted up with red paint and green curtains to give an Italian feel. Fresh flowers adorned small tables, an aroma somewhere between hot pesto, fried meats and tomatoes engaged the senses as a capable and highly articulate waiter led us to our table. The staff were all genuine Italian and the food accordingly excellent.

Watching Val as the night went on gave me great pleasure. She relaxed and smiled broader than ever, the creases at the corners of her eyes the only clue to her age. To compliment this, her figure and posture gave the impression of a woman at least a decade younger. Being childless must have contributed to her lack of grey hair, or other signs of ageing brought on by the trials of Motherhood. With her hair hanging gorgeous, dark against bare shoulders sprinkled with pale freckles, she appeared ravishing.

"You're looking great tonight Val; you've got all the waiters eyeing you up." I said with a smile whilst refilling her glass with the house red.

"Thanks Dan, that's nice of you." She smiled then ran her hands down her curves. "Yeah, nice outfit this, ain't it?"

"Really sexy Val, especially with the boots", I winked.

After skipping dessert, we enjoyed a strong expresso each as I settled the bill. Walking out, the moon shone bright in a clear, star-filled sky and the night felt young. "Fancy a drive to the coast?" I asked, wrapping an arm around her shoulder and pulling her close as we walked towards the Humber.

"Yeah alright, where you got in mind?"

"Somewhere quiet, where we can park by the sea."

"I hope you don't expect me to have it off with you in the car!"

"Of course not!" Slapping her bum to emphasise my exclamation. "Cheeky! I only fancy parking up and looking out to sea, that's all."

Within the hour we were sat in the moonlight, on a stone bench on the beach front. Smoking cigarettes together in contemplative silence. We knew the issue on both our minds. But neither of us wished to disturb our peace by bringing Sean's name up. The cigarette smoke helped me relax and focus on what to say. Stubbing it out, I looked at Val directly. "Everything alright at home? Anymore unexpected visits?" She exhaled smoke with measured coolness, then put the stub out with a scrape of her heel before answering. Very considered, I noted.

"Listen Dan, I know you mean well but its best if you leave Sean to me. He's nothing but trouble, always has been. Ever since we were kids, nothing but trouble."

"He must be for you to have never mentioned him to me. I hope I haven't made things worse."

"I don't think they could be much worse Dan." These words she said with uncharacteristic softness. A rare flicker of vulnerability. However, she changed tack in the next breath. "Let's leave it, eh? I didn't want to bring Sean into our space, he's not here and he won't be dropping in out the blue like the other week. I've made sure of that."

So, Val had seen her brother since his unexpected visit. I did as she asked and let it go. We didn't mention him again. Yet inside, my mind teemed. Killing Sean had now evolved into a matter of honour.

Everything about Sean told me we'd been pre-ordained to meet. Without CB radio, or The Mouth, or my act as Dan Turner, none of this could have occurred. Our paths would never have crossed. Fate brought our lives to coincide at a time quickened to bring about a most unfortunate and violent chain of events. The paradox of Dan leading me to kill Sean exposes the real motives behind my behaviour.

All to sate my appalling, private demands. To commit murder upon those whom I deemed justifiable. However, in Sean's case there were complications, to say the least. Despite there existing no evidence to suggest Sean had been responsible for any loss of life, the maniac within my bosom brushed this inconvenient variance aside. Sean had to go.

KILLING GLEE

Rays of sunlight shone down out of a clear blue sky. Through the leaves of a twin-trunked Silver Birch, dappling into a cascade of shifting half-shadows and light-beams onto Val's front garden. Bright light piercing the light cotton of the short blue dress she wore, highlighting her pleasing figure, whilst also laying a shining band of radiance onto her dark, seductive locks. Wisps of Lavender and Camomile came and went on a gentle, late-summer breeze. Val knelt on a little cushion, weeding through the borders. I put on a pair of thick gloves she'd laid out for me, picked up her secateurs and set about the dog-roses growing across an arched gateway to the lawn.

"Hey! Don't chop them off anywhere. Take your time", Val called across. I turned back to her with the secateurs raised and open, waving them with a limp-wristed camp style. A pathetic attempt at what I thought Dan would do to be humorous.

"I know." My voice a few pitches higher than usual in some inane effort of stupidity. "I'll just be taking the hips for syrup."

"Make sure you do." She said, unamused, turning back to her weeding.

'Stop trying to be Dan you idiot.'
'What should I do then?'
'Just fucking be him.'

Over the course of several weeks, Val became evermore distant. Little things, but intimate and telling nonetheless. A certain degree of stiffness entered our relationship. Conversations were less natural. Close to being stilted at times. Since his unexpected return, Val's inerrant brother occupied her mind. Seeming to come and go as he pleased. Yet he made sure never to coincide with my visits. The fact Val perceived my sorry deceptions as easy as her brother had, never occurred to me.

Sean must have been asking questions. He may even have known some notable members of London's underworld, who of course would never have heard of Dan Turner. Doubts were creeping in for Val. Old instincts of mine were aroused, prickling at her uncharacteristic silences.

The need to hold onto Val, in order to play Dan, stirred me into this calamitous train of thought. Motivating me to find reprieve. A pitiful attempt to escape myself. This self-deceptive, delusional thinking taught me a harsh lesson; - There is no escape.

'This will work. It's a good plan.'

'I hope so.'

'You need to kill again. The idea is clever. Sean will take the bait.'

'This one could rid me of my need to kill.'

'Ha! A cure? For You? Intriguing!'

There I sat, comfortable and warm in Dan's Humber Sceptre. Heading towards Val's. The car shook as wild elements ran amok outside, battering us with heavy rain and gale-force gusts of wind. This type of weather had been going on for days. Therefore, in anticipation of bad road conditions, I'd set off early. Driving from Bottesford with languid serenity, being as polite and accommodating to other road users as possible, taking plenty of time. This provided the opportunity to rehearse my story for Val along the way. With only a few miles of the journey left to go, the circumstances were no different from those I'd left behind. Slate-grey skies from end to end. We were in for one of those week-long soaks which keep England forever green.

On the front passenger seat sat a sleek, dark red leather case. From time to time, I rested my left hand upon it, enjoying caressing the smooth warmth of the fine leather covering and the silky Rosewood carrying handle. Everything about the little case exuded quality and craftmanship of the maximum order for the materials used in its construction. Although perfect in function, its form's discreet excellence induced the most spontaneous and grateful admiration. Beautiful and bespoke, a unique jeweller's case. Within it were a number of one kilo gold bars of significant value. Some had been cast and were crude in comparison to the others, which had been minted in Austria. All however were pure high-grade gold and together worth a small fortune. More than enough to buy a nice detached house in a quiet leafy suburb in the Home Counties. Plenty enough to tempt Sean into ripping me off, creating an opportunity to be alone with, then dispose of him.

'Is the irony of this situation not apparent to you?'

'Not now.'

'A murder to end your murders? Fresh blood to end the craving?'

'Perhaps.'

'Only time will tell.'

'Even if...it will never be like it was. I'll be in control.'

'Your confidence is admirable.'

Val wasn't expecting me. Therefore, I parked on the lane outside her yard, hoping she'd soon become aware of my presence. Anticipating her to appear on foot to open the gate and wave me in. I stepped out, popped the boot to get an umbrella, opened it then lit a cigarette. Beneath the tall Cedars and broad Willows of the lane, the wind and rain were mild enough to smoke in a reasonably civilised manner. The calm before the storm. A moment to focus on being Dan Turner one hundred percent.

Val came into view. Arms folded, walking fast to open the wooden five-bar gate before gesturing at me to enter. Wearing flat shoes and short-legged jeans topped by a chequered blouse and hand-knitted cardigan, she looked sweeter than ever.

'She does have a fine figure.'

'Behave.'

Val spoke whilst closing the gate, as soon as I stepped from the car; - "What the bloody hell you doing turning up here like this Dan?"

"Sorry Val, don't like to surprise you, but I couldn't call ahead. Bit of an emergency, that sort of thing."

"You'd better not have brought the law along behind you!" Her lips were tight and the words spat tersely, surprising me.

"Listen, if you've got company or you're expecting someone, I'll just go."

"Of course I bloody haven't! Don't be like that. You should know I don't have anyone else around here Dan. I have enough trouble off Sean over you, thank you very much."

"What kind of trouble?" Asking to redirect the focus.

"Nothing I can't handle. He doesn't like you, doesn't trust you."

"And he tells you not to trust me either? Is that it?"

"Yes. But Sean says that about everyone. He doesn't trust anyone he doesn't know or hasn't been vouched for by one of his friends. He gets involved in some heavy stuff. You really don't want to know." By this point I'd left the car on the lane and we were walking into her rear porchway. She led the way and picked a pack of cigarettes from a shelf inside and turned, blocking the door.

Cool as a Lee Van Cleef character, Val struck a wooden Bryant and May match with poetic aplomb. She lit the cigarette, narrowed, scrutinising eyes boring into my own. The smell of sulphur pleasant to my nostrils as she waved the flaming match out. Inhaling slow and deep on the cigarette before exhaling upwards to her left, she glanced down at the little case swinging in my grip.

"So, what you got there then? What's this all about? You know not to bloody well turn up out the blue. You're lucky Sean int' here. He wouldn't have been happy for you to turn up without my prior knowledge." To say her attitude was hostile would be stretching it, but not by much.

"It's Sean I'd like to talk to."

"Sean won't want to see *you*, take my word for it. I asked you what you've got there Dan." Again, Val's words were stand-offish and suspicious.

"Something valuable, which I wasn't expecting to have. If you get me. Please Val, we need to be indoors if you want to see what I've got. Tell you what, if you don't agree that Sean will be interested once I let you see what's in here, I'll bugger off and try to think of something else. I wouldn't have come to you like this without good reason." Her eyes continued to hold mine and she seemed not to blink either. Then she put the smouldering, half-smoked cigarette into a small porcelain ashtray, turned on her heels and said;

"I hope this is worth it Dan."

We made our way through the kitchen and hallway into her living room. Although Val slept with her dogs on the boat in a private mooring at the end of her garden, she used the old cottage for everything else. Val pulled the curtains fully open which let in wide beams of sunlight across brown rugs covering the red-tiled floor. She sat in an upholstered armchair and motioned for me to sit on a matching three-seater sofa at right angles to her. A sturdy oak coffee table occupied the space in front of the sofa so I pulled it closer after sitting down. Placing the case onto the table with care, I sat back before speaking.

"Now, none of this was planned Val, you got to understand." Holding my hands out palm up to her. "All I know is someone needed a motor getting rid of, a.s.a.p. Just like all the rest, yeah?" Val shrugged. A non-committal acknowledgement to continue. "Picked the car up a couple of nights ago. Took her straight to my lock-up south of the river, where they stay a while before being taken to be crushed or burnt out. Last night as I was doing the usual sweep over for any contraband, this little number turned up. Beneath the passenger seat. Somehow it had found its way under there so snug no-one noticed. I just want rid for a good price. In case someone comes asking. I'll deny all knowledge if anyone does, but it's doubtful they will anyway. Those involved have all left the country with the rest of their haul. At least that's what I heard." Opening the case and turning it to face Val whilst speaking these last words. Of course, I knew 'they' wouldn't. There being no 'they'. The case and its contents had cost me a substantial sum of money in several legal transactions. It all belonged to me.

"Fucking hell Dan!" The exclamation erupted from Val's mouth before she had a chance to catch it. Then, slender fingers went to feel the glistering objects which captivated her gaze so much. "Can I touch one? Please Dan, they're beautiful. Never seen anything like these before."

"Yeah of course, here, this one." Sincerity filled my reply as I pointed to a minted bar of particular magnetism, knowing how people are affected by the sight of an abundance of real gold. The substance has a mesmeric power all of its own. I'd seen it before and experienced it myself. Val felt it, right there and then. Once opened, the interior of the case resembled a ladies' fine jewellery box, exquisite in dark orange silk and embossed gold stitching. Within this setting the bullion appeared enchanting.

Beneath the calm demeanour, my scheming mind gloated. Val had bitten the bait and swallowed it whole. Hook, line, sinker. A hint of copper, reminiscent of warm blood, tanged on my taste-buds as flashbacks of previous murders leapt onto the screen within my mind, triggered by eager anticipation of slaying Sean.

Val waited as I took the indicated bar from the box and place it in her palm. Then walked over to the window with the gleaming chunk of gold held out before her. Flashes of light bounced around the walls and ceiling as the bar reflected the sunlight angling in through the windows.

"Some weight to it, this is proper gold bullion, must be worth thousands."

"You reckon? Maybe all kosher, from a dealer and all that Val. But not as hot as it is right now. Not to me. I'd be happy to sort out a price for them all with your brother, if you can help get him interested. There's five-hundred for you out of it if he takes the case. He must know someone who could help him out with this sort of thing, surely? I mean, he's not going to want to touch it unless he can make a few quid. With his connections, he should be able to get a decent price. A better one than I could, at least here up North. I can't possibly try and flog this in London. No way. Tell him all I want is ten grand and they're all his, no questions asked. That wood and leather case alone must be worth a grand Val, look at it."

"I know Dan, I know. I can see that. Sean won't want to be all pally with you though, you have to understand the way he is. Maybe later, when he's made a good few quid. But if he does like the sound of it, please, do me a favour and let him do all the talking."

"Don't worry. If he's willing to take this lot off my hands for ten grand cash, he can do as much talking as he likes." Oh, Sean would like the sound of it alright. I could hear the cogs whirring in Val's head as she scanned the contents of the case, rapidly ascertaining the value of the gold must far exceed the ten thousand I wanted.

"I'm not sure how much gold is worth these days but there's plenty here", she chimed, placing the bar back inside with a clink. "I don't know about you but I could do with a coffee. Fancy one?"

"Yes please, that'd be lovely Val, thanks."

"I can see we need to talk", she added before filling the kettle and placing it on the stove, lighting the gas ring with a match. Val's dogs were all curled up together on an old blanket beside the stove. She looked again into the case and sat down whilst the water boiled. "Do you really not know where that thing came from?"

"Like I told you Val, the case was in the car. The people I deal with don't tell me anything, only where to pick each motor up. And that's over a public telephone. Nothing is done face-to-face if it doesn't have to be. There's an envelope of cash left as payment for me beneath the spare wheel or under the carpet. From time to time a few bits of contraband have turned up in one or two of the cars. Unless I pick up some information off the grapevine down there, I don't know anything. And its best I don't!" Allowing the pent-up emotions in me to come out in character worked, it made me sound sincere enough to wind Val up.

"Calm yourself down Dan!" She retaliated in kind. "Don't be raising your voice to me in my own home!"

"I am calm. I need you to help me, please." Speaking quieter and slower, keeping her focused on me. Meanwhile Val continued with making the drinks, with the usual clinking and clattering of pots and cutlery involved. Throwing myself fully into character I let the words flow out. "Sorry for raising my voice Val but this is a great deal. Alright, Sean might have to do some work and wait a while to get anywhere near the true value of the gold, but he could also choose to pass it on and double his money within a couple of weeks too. As long as we can shift this soon because I cannot hold onto it myself for very long. Just tell him about it. He might not like me, maybe he has good reason to be suspicious of everyone he doesn't know but either way I am not working for the police nor am I out to set anyone up." Val remained composed, thinking, looking at me, then at the gold bars and the case. She handed me a hot mug of coffee and we sat back in our seats, each of us letting out a sigh. I'd been on the go myself all morning, necessitating the coffee.

"It's a big deal Dan, dropping this on him out of the blue, it will get his heckles up." She stared right at me; "If he smells a rat, he'll skin you alive there and then, no questions asked. You sure you want to meet up with him?"

"If he's interested, I want to see him alone, somewhere private. If he's got anyone else with him, the deals off."

"Christ almighty will you calm down Dan! You can't go making demands like that of my brother, he'll only get the hump even more."

"Maybe, but that's it. Anyway, I reckon he'll be alright with that. I'm no threat to him, he'll meet me. If he's got all the cash on him, he gets all the gold. Simple enough deal. Do you think he can get the cash?

"Yeah, he'll have it."

"I mean within a couple of days?"

"Yes, if he wants to spend it, he'll dig the cash out from one of his stashes somewhere. You might get a few old notes, mind."

"Couldn't care less as long as they're still legal tender", I winked. Val smiled back. We were getting on again, despite a little tension. However, all my focus remained on The Hit.

Drinking the strong, creamy coffee gave me a few seconds to think. Best to keep pushing, but gently. "You know this is the first time I've actually calmed down since finding this lot. At first all-sorts of ideas went through my mind. Coming here and chancing it with you was my best option Val. Most of all I had to get it out of London. Getting in touch over the CB was no good, not for this."

"It still don't make it a good idea Dan, Sean's un-fucking-predictable enough at the best of times."

"But this lot is obviously worth a mint, right? It's obvious to you, it will be just as obvious to him."

"Yes, once he's got his own greedy fucking hands on it Dan, that's the problem. He'll try and only give you half the money, then he'll disappear again for another six months. He's only back to do some dirty business. And I can't be doing with being stuck between the pair of you. I don't know what he's got himself into now, but I do know he's involved with some foreigners. For Sean to be back over here, with a warrant and serious charges still hanging over him, must mean a lot of money is involved. It'd have to be. A lot of money."

"He should have enough to help us out then."

"Help *you* out Dan. Even if you gave me half the cash, Sean wouldn't see it as helping me out at all. He could take care of any money problems I might run into himself, except I'm not that daft. He'll know straight away this is all your idea. There's no way he'd believe I came to you for help with money."

"That's not what I meant Val. Your right, this is my problem. But what can I do with a case of gold bullion? If I'd never met your brother in the first place coming here to get something for it wouldn't ever have been an option, would it?"

An inner chuckle ran through me at the sheer front of my rhetoric. As Dan, the statement was untrue. As myself it aided the drama of the situation, keeping up my veil of deception.

The truth happened to be simple, brutal. Once again, the hunt had begun. Sean was my next Target and like a homing missile, I had locked on for The Hit. Beneath the earnest but deceptive conversation with Val, my mind over-flowed with all the possible outcomes of my endeavour. Full of evil intent, murderous in thought, cunning with subtle manipulation.

"No. I don't suppose you would have brought all this here if you hadn't met Sean, or if I hadn't told you about his life."

"I don't know much more about him than a decent copper could tell at a glance Val. Be honest, he doesn't do himself any favours. Besides, like I keep saying, I want rid of it. Can't take this back down South with me so it will have to go one way or another this week. If Sean can take the whole case off me without any fuss I don't care if he trebles his money overnight."

Had to keep pushing the 'limited time' sales pitch, it added authenticity. And the costs didn't concern me. All I really cared about was getting a chance to kill again.

After two days, a call to 'Vienna Rose' over the CB to push for an answer seemed reasonable. Not to Val though. Perhaps she smelled a rat even then. Speaking over the CB radio, even without resorting to code, we had to refrain from using our own or any other person's real name. We created ways to skirt around them.

"Call whats-his-name up and tell him I want to make the deal this week. But only with him. I can bring the merchandise straight to wherever he wants." I said as "Dynamite".

"What do you mean call him? I can't just get hold of him like that." Val's voice crackled back through the receiver.

"Okay, well what can you do then?"

"I can leave a message with one of his contacts, but I don't know when he'll get it." Val didn't seem certain, as if she knew more. Of course she did. But why the resistance? Why the hesitancy?

"Come on, there's got to be a better way to contact him."

"You reckon? What makes you say that? He probably don't know where he's gonna be from one day to the next himself! So how am I supposed to know?" She sounded irritated, distant and unwilling to commit.

"Okay, Just do whatever you can then, please. I need to get this stuff off my hands."

"All I can promise is to make sure he knows your needs are urgent. After that it's up to him. The minute I hear anything, I'll be putting a call out for you, so keep tuned in on here at the usual times. I'll use frequency one-nine until you respond, then we'll switch channels."

"Okay, understood. But be sure to tell him how much money he can make off this merchandise and the quality of it. Then he'll respond quickly."

"I told you already I will", Val quipped.

"Alright, remember to tell him I want to do the deal in person. Just me and him."

"As you say, but no promises he'll want to go through with it." With that we broke the connection and I clicked off the CB.

Val's words fell into my plan. She didn't want to contact Sean on my behalf but the value of the gold bullion spoke for itself. Sean would think Dan wanted to become acquainted with him in a criminal way, then be unable to resist the opportunity to rip Dan off. Crushing what he saw as an attempt at bridge-building by his sister's latest flame. Taking the gold, humiliating Dan, forcing him to stay away from Val. The problem Sean faced being he would be meeting me instead. Dan couldn't be there. Not for long.

DEATH OF THE APOSTATE

The day arrived. The eagerly anticipated day Sean and I would be alone. The meeting place, a ruin situated in a woodland several miles inland from the Norfolk coastline. The trees, Birch, Ash and Sycamore, were neither large nor very old. Seeds blown by wind or carried by animals and birds had self-set over the years, to cover the remains of an old temporary army training camp from the First World War.

Driving there in Dan's Humber, once again. Using detailed directions as a guide, I drove onto a private road off a country lane. Through a mossy gate hidden in a dip, onto an unpaved track into the sparse but large expanse of woodland. A mile in, a clearing marked the site of the former parade ground. Although this too had its own green cloak shrouding the hard concrete surface beneath. Small shrubs and heaths formed lines along the joins and cracks in the old concrete. Between these a coat of light grass grew on top of inches of built-up mossy detritus. Down the East side of this old square, one building yet remained, standing as solid testament to the locations former service. A long, single-storey concrete block house, possibly once the showers and other areas of ablutions, stood almost hidden by overgrowth and trees. An area perhaps an eighth of an acre in front of this building remained clear of overgrowth due to being in use of some kind. One of Sean's places, no doubt. Approached from two directions as the lane continued on through with access from the far end. This is the way Sean came from, as we'd agreed.

He drove up in a red 1969 Ford Capri GT. A few years old but still looking good enough to seem incongruous in the leafy setting. When Sean stepped out and approached, for the first time I realised he stood at least two inches taller than myself. The crowded headroom of Val's glasshouse, overflowing with vines, had concealed her brother's full height to me. Also, powerful, full of confidence, striding fast, determination carved into his rugged features.

'First chance you get. No messing.'
'I know. First chance I get.'
'Watch him, he means business.'
'I mean it more.'

Sean strode right up to, then past me. With scant regard he half glanced over his shoulder, saying in harsh, abrupt words; - "Well, come on then", without breaking step. I followed him into the bare blockhouse, the insides of which were clear of growth, dry and windswept. Only the concrete frame of the building remained, all the woodwork, doorframes, windows, gutters, etc, were long gone. He'd already turned to face me as I stepped into this enclosed space with him.

"I've got five fucking grand for you. Take it or leave it. You say you need to get rid of that gold?" He pointed over my shoulder towards the Humber, keeping his finger up a few seconds whilst glaring and pushing his face towards where his finger pointed. I remained facing him, maintaining a curious expression, until he dropped his hand, trying not to acknowledge the awkwardness my lack of reaction created. So, Sean really thought Dan had come along with the gold. He was nowhere near as astute as his sister proved to be.

'That's presumptive of him!'
'Very trusting.'
'His overconfidence is clear. Wait for it, he's got something to say.'
'It won't make any difference. He's already dead.'

I nodded at Sean in way of response, "Yeah." Within, Dan ceased to exist. The sensation took me by surprise. Being Dan got in the way. Keeping up any sort of act rapidly slipped from my desire and control.

"Tell you what", Sean blurted, aggression abundant in his tone; - "Your gonna take this five grand and fuck off. I never want to hear about you again. You can fuck off away from my sister and just keep going. I don't like you, Danny boy. Did you *really* think you could get in with me, like this? Forget it. I don't like you and never will. There's something about you that winds me up. Now, go on, get the gold and bring it here, to me."

'Let him keep talking'
'Until when?'
'When you've had enough.'
'I've had more than enough.'

Stationary, eyes locked, I stood impassive in the stony doorway. Blocking the light. A silhouette of doom. Here only for him. Several heartbeats went by. I relaxed whilst Sean tensed up. The air between us crackled, charged with intense emotion. Sean went to say something, but checked himself before speaking. Micro-expressions rippled beneath his features, as potent thoughts and considerations ran amok in his frantic mind. Satisfaction coursed through me as fear took charge of him. Fear he could not hide. The veil had been lifted. We were as naked before one another. My act evaporated into mist as his act crumbled into dust. The time to be real had come.

"You're right Sean, there is something about me, isn't there? But you see, the me you think you know, well he doesn't exist. Dan Turner isn't real. But I am. And you know it, don't you, Seany boy? So, how now?" Voicing these words in my usual tone and manner, not the more light-hearted way Dan had spoken, affected Sean. But the dullard only had one way of responding.

"Oh yeah is that supposed to fucking scare me? I couldn't give a fuck what you call yourself or why. Just get that fucking gold before I take it from you and leave you here." Brave words. Yet the slightest of quavering in his voice belied the rising dread beneath Sean's flippant courage.

"You know that's not going to happen Sean. Though I admire your bravado. What is going to happen is I'm going to kill you. I've killed many men before you, you're not special. But you are perfect for me. You see it in my eyes, don't you? A psycho-killer, coming for you." Finishing my threat by quoting a recent top forty chart hit. Corny, but true. I still love that song.

Sean could not speak. Standing dumbfounded before me, frozen. No quips, bravado or any more dismissive aggression, which had been my expectation. My words rang so true his blood ran cold at the sound of them. He had plenty of instinct, realising he'd been absolutely correct not to trust me. All this flooded through his senses. Not having to think whether or not I spoke the truth. He could feel it. A shiver ran through him and his pupils dilated. Then I noticed the hammering in my own chest. It shook me, whilst Sean swayed on his feet. Sharing a moment of such profound recognition, we paused.

Perhaps a dozen hard heartbeats went by. Yet, the absolute stillness of those few seconds shall linger forever. A sensation of greater intensity than any other in my experience. This had become personal. As the occasion unfolded, a realization struck my mind. I was feeling the greatest rush of them all. In that moment, a voice said this *had* to be my best kill. These thoughts distilled latent savagery into over-driven barbarism with tremendous rapidity. Fuelling the aggression. Building pressure within, to an explosive level.

The moment felt beautiful. Sean shrunk before me. On the surface he kept some composure but my words had chilled him to the bone. Blood drained from his face as adrenaline burst into his system. Instinct told me within another heartbeat he would move, one way or the other. He could now see what confronted him. Worse than a cold-blooded killer. Sean had my blood boiling. I wanted to eat him alive.

⸺◈⸺

Condensed hatred surged into fervent deed. A volcanic detonation of murderous intent propelled me. As a pack of hungry dogs would an old chicken trapped in a yard. Bad intentions took hold. Stepping forward, a short, hard punch from my left fist to Sean's Adam's apple got me in close. His left arm snapped with little effort up his back as I slipped behind him. With a gargled screech, the bully dropped onto his fat face. Shock stopped him struggling as much once I'd gouged his eyes out, but breath still gasped out from him in hard, noisy bursts. Unable to scream due to his crushed larynx, he squawked and grunted beneath me. I gripped his hairy eyebrows and with some effort ripped the top of his face up onto the front of his skull. Sitting astride his shoulders provided enormous leverage. Thick, well-manicured fingernails dug deep into flesh. With my knee in the back of his neck, it took several violent, jerking tugs before the epidermal surface separated from the muscle and fibres beneath, but once this happened momentum did the rest. At this point his back broke, somewhere in the ribcage simultaneous to his neck snapping at the base. Manicured fingernails filled with a disgusting mix of blood, flesh and fat. My knuckles never went so white, such was the force of the grip and effort employed in this particular manoeuvre. Sean still lived, just about. Although unconscious, hideous snorting huffs and wheezes testified to some life still being left in the man.

Getting up, I turned and left him lying there in the dark, empty concrete room. He'd be another cold corpse soon enough. Walking back to the car, heartrate slowing, the emotions of the moment inundated me. No remorse, no regret. Though dazed, elated, magnificent and victorious. I felt like the only man on Earth. Alone with God. Pure. Unadulterated. Clean. Clear. Sterile as diamond. The Wrath of God, in service of his Creator. My best ever service. The Best.

The aftermath began later that day. Those moments after slaying Sean are some of the most lucid of my entire life. Whether he kicked his legs, or had any struggle left in him at all as I tore his face off, is a detail excluded from my recall. Yet the temperature, scents, humidity, wind and natural sounds I experienced for the immediate minutes afterwards, remain forever indelible in my mind.

Stepping outside into the forest air felt good. Wind blew hard enough to sway the tree tops against each other, creating creaking and groaning from the larger branches. Memory remains so vivid for those few minutes. Wind thrashed browning bracken whilst whispering between dry grasses, announcing a turn in the weather as a cold front moved eastwards across the Fens towards the Norfolk coastline. The light from the sky had gone from the blue-white of earlier, to grey-greyer as the sun became obscured by gathering storm-clouds.

'How apt.' For once there was no response to the voice, mocking from the back of my head in its rasping, cruel version of my own natural voice.

Stiff limbs marked the short walk back over to the Sceptre. Fingers sore from exertion, fumbling. Looking at my hands, a shudder ran through me. Dripping blood and sticky with gore. This instinctive reaction brought the realisation of just how acrimonious and savage the affair had become. Some loose soil formed by rabbits digging for roots helped clean the worst of it from my throbbing fingers. Broad leaves from nearby undergrowth brought the rest off.

When clean enough, I got in the car and started driving. Not stopping at all, I drove for over an hour before pulling up in a secluded spot. In a daze of sorts, overcome by the release of so much aggression. Sunbeams broke through clouds in the rear-view mirror, indicating North had been the direction of this auto-pilot drive.

The murder scene flashed into my mind's eye. So much mess. The whole event being entirely dissimilar to my previous works. The personal nature of this Hit unleashed deep levels of barbarity. An incredible cognizance. An ecstasy of vicious glee emanated from my heart.

I drove for hours that senseless Sunday. Thoughts swirling in the aftermath of Sean's pitiless demise. The idea of ever pretending to be Dan again began to appal me. Any notion of returning to Val dwindled into nothingness. Desire to be Dan, or even partake in any of that little charade in my life at all, now seemed an utter impossibility.

'Sadist.'

'Fuck Off. I control my mind.'

'Of course you do.'

The voice taunted. It knew my guilt. Val. How would she find out? When would the news be brought to her? And by whom? Who would find Sean? Someone would happen along the grisly scene sooner or later.

STRANGE WEEK

Monday. Dumped the Humber in Sheffield and took an early train back to The Smoke. London life took over and subsequent days went by with ease. Engrossed in working on my business portfolio, whilst tempting investments involved several meetings during the latter half of that week.

After months of waiting and making excuses, Mary did not have a single dull moment. She seemed very happy too. Now able to make good on lost time. Once again, when alone, I could feel that Mary clearly knew I'd been involved in a way much more than casual, with another woman. Although curiosity, rather than jealousy exuded from her. This intrigued me. Mary had never before shown interest in any of my private affairs, except for our own.

Some of Mary's mannerisms were without doubt more than mere affection. The way she spoke to me. The habits she employed to ensure our intimacy remained untainted by emotional friction, whilst still encompassing a fiery passion. A great desire to be out with Mary in public, as a couple, as I'd done numerous times that year with Val, overcame me.

"Mary, where would you like me to take you?" I asked on the Tuesday morning, as we drank coffee and went over notes from the day before in my office.

"What do you mean?" Answering my question with one of her own as she hadn't fully caught onto what I was asking. She had her eyes fixed on some details in the paperwork open on the desk.

"Out. Where would you like to go?"

"You mean on a date?" Now she looked up and gave me her full attention, incredulity colouring her words.

"Of course, but no expense spared. Go up to the West End if you like."

"Oh, Sam, that would be lovely!" Mary blushed, chest and face flushing with a rush of redness. She stood up from the desk in excitement. "I've got just the thing to wear!" Beaming her delight with a broad smile.

"Hmm, sounds intriguing."

"It's a little two-piece outfit I picked up in Chelsea. You'll like it", she said, full of assurance.

"I don't doubt that for a minute. Where'd you fancy going, got anywhere in mind?"

"Well, I have been reading all about that Jesus Christ Superstar musical, never been to see that one. Would love to see it. I haven't been to the theatre at all since my sister Sarah left to go and live in Milan."

"Oh yes, I remember you mentioning that. How is she?"

"Sarah's fine, she always is. Bit of trouble with the house when they moved in, something about the insurance, nothing serious, apart from that, Sarah's all good. Now, are you taking me to the West End or what?" She asked, placing one hand on her hip.

"I suppose I am. Two tickets it is then." I said, voice full of cheer. Mary straightened, still surprised.

"Really Sam? Oh, I'd love that so much! But when for?"

"Whenever you like, as long as it's this week." I asserted.

"Oh, don't worry Sam, it will be!" She grinned, shivering her shoulders and clenching her hands with excitement.

———◇———

Time and money spent spoiling Mary provided immense pleasure. Each moment felt effortless, natural, relaxed. We enjoyed the Jesus Christ musical she'd been so keen to see on the Wednesday evening. Enjoying a front row, balcony seat. Her eyes gleamed with joy as she took in the polished performances and songs. Albeit for myself, watching Mary so engrossed and happy provided far more gratification than any West End show ever could.

Mary and I enjoyed these brief, yet pacific days in each other's company. Bereft of thoughts concerning Val, Sean, or anything else to do with Dan Turner. But this idyllic oblivion could not last. Something gnawed away in a dark corner of my mind. Something other than guilt. Dispatching Sean had felt incredible. Yet the gnawing persisted. Somehow my actions had caused an affect which remained beyond my discernment. Outside the reach of distinct perception. Unknown factors had been influenced by Sean's gory ending. This feeling intensified throughout the week.

A sensation haunted me. As if Val's presence hovered close by. Nightmares disturbed my sleep. Unease shaded my heart. Following a particular intense and troubling night on the Thursday, Val's visage flashed into my mind's eye upon waking, alone in my hotel room. The vision unnerved me. Having lost my appetite for breakfast, I asked Mary to clear my diary for the following week. An urge to return to the Fens listen in on the CB and monitor for Val's voice, compelled this decision.

<hr />

Saturday morning. Took a maroon coloured, Deluxe Edition, Austin 3000cc BMC Series from a lock-up in South Bermondsey. Located under a brick railway arch on the South London Line. One among a row of eleven. All owned by one of my property businesses. Nine of the other ten being let out to a variety of small business owners.

A handy motor. Like the Humber, the Austin being one of a dozen or so cars I kept in storage in London and The Midlands. She'd been due a proper spin for over a year. After making sure to fill the tank with four-star before leaving the city, I then nailed the throttle to stay ahead of the weekend traffic.

The car thrummed along the broad roads North of London. At one point the needle even tipped beyond 120mph. However, the Austin remained rock solid. A beautiful drive, mesmerising, losing a couple of hours in serene bliss. The soothing trundle and constant pace funnelling and crushing all thought into the present. Denying doubt, fear, or any other form of timidity to disturb manifest intention. The quality of the car's interior, the warmth of the wooden steering wheel and the sweeping roads combined to ease my mind into a continuum of fulfilment. Just myself, the road and the machine.

Brightening skies ensured the morning grew less dark further North. Taking in the scenery whenever possible helped clear opaque thoughts. Tired eyes being treated to sunbeams blasting down at steep angles between ice-cream clouds. Illuminating the rolling fields and vales, themselves dotted with dark copses, which seemed to fill much of Cambridgeshire as I passed through it.

My constructive mood evaporated as the familiar roads of West Norfolk rolled beneath the wheels. Once within ten miles of Val's nearest village, a decent lay-by looked inviting with privacy and space. Time to park up and take stock.

Only a week had passed since killing Sean. Yet the gruesome events of that day seemed distant, as if they'd occurred in a previous lifetime. The glove box closed with a satisfactory click as I took out a fresh Cuban cigar. There I sat smoking. Considering it all. Being Dan Turner now seemed like a dream. All of it.

'Even the graphic murder of your lover's brother?'

'Not now.'

'Oh dear. Those nightmares are making you impatient.'

'Just stop.'

'Does any of it seem real to you yet?'

'Val does. She's real.'

'Dream on. Val may be real but not to you. Not yet. Only the murder was real. The real you.'

'Val doesn't know me at all does she?'

'Maybe more than you think.'

Whilst in London, the distance and distractions had closed a door in my mind to the Dan affair. All the deceit, nastiness and mess had been put beneath a heavy lid, screwed down, airtight. All except Val. Whatever else may have been on my mind, there she remained. A feeling, a knowing, a nagging. Not just my mind. My heart. Val had earned more than my trust and respect.

A good woman. Val did not deserve to be left so cold in grief and uncertainty. Instinct, the immutable barometer of truth, stated that certain earnest considerations had arisen. Information as yet unbeknown pulled with irresistible petition upon fraught heartstrings. Something was up and I had to find out. To walk away and never be Dan again, as planned, became an impossibility.

Thus, in attendance of these thoughts, I sat. Parked up, enjoying the portly cigar, mulling it all over. Wondering what Val knew about her brother's demise. And more importantly, what she thought my involvement in it might have been. Were the Law involved? Would Val have gone to the police? No way to be certain. Nor whether she blamed me, or wanted me dead. If the truth had become apparent to her, indeed she would.

Doubt got to me. An old adage came back, "if in doubt, leave it out." Started the car and drove straight towards the cottage in Bottesford, rather than pay Val a visit. On arrival there an hour later, I discovered the place ransacked.

Articles had been destroyed rather than looted. Everything inside, all the fittings and fixtures; doors, cupboards, drawers, appliances. Smashed, broken, despoiled. Food, stored in tins, jars and sacks, had been liberally distributed throughout. Creating a conflicting miasma of sweet fragrances and repulsive odours, as some edibles corrupted faster than others. Gagging the throat. Furniture lay slashed, splintered and broken in useless, impeding heaps. Although, whoever had done this, had left all the CB equipment undamaged. This one room remained untarnished and welcoming amid the chaos of wanton destruction. It appeared an obvious message. Someone wanted to speak to me.

HIDDEN HANDS

T he cottage slipped from my interest and had to go. Within a month it had been stripped out, refitted and put on the market. However, the days following the break-in saw me busy with the CB apparatus. Re-locating various parts to the Transit van. Purchasing extra car batteries for additional power. These changes boosted the range. Enabling me to pick up Val's signal from greater distances.

The Transit I'd moved a month earlier. From a public car-park in Boston to a lumber yard next to the River Trent in Newark, Nottinghamshire. The owner having sought my investment on a racehorse some years prior. Things turned out to be lucrative for all involved and we'd maintained an excellent rapport since. We exchanged a wad of cash for a key to a padlock. This opened the gate to a small section of his yard. A dank place, with a roof of moss-covered, corrugated asbestos. The moss, twigs and leaves being produced by several huge Beech trees, which towered and spread above the entire area, keeping it private and secluded, perfect for my work.

I shifted location to a hotel on the outskirts of Leicester. From there, driving the Austin out to the Transit each day. Then driving around South-Lincolnshire using the boosted-up rig in the van to scan for Val's voice. Or "Vienna Rose" as the CB community knew her. Using an Ordnance Survey map proved invaluable. A location on relatively high ground west of Peterborough offered the best reception levels for miles around. Although following a few days of passive listening with no results, a change of approach became necessary.

I had to join in with the general CB chat. Putting my handle, "Dynamite", out there. Hoping Val might be tuned in herself.

Mentioning "Vienna Rose" to anyone who would listen. Asking them to pass on the message I wished to contact her. Ensuring everyone knew I'd be tuned in listening for her on frequency one-nine each evening.

⋙◈⋘

Within a week Val came on air and we chose a channel to speak on. This frequency open but only accessible to anyone within range. Things were so fraught we spoke plainly, without using any accepted CB interjections at all. Val seemed concerned. "You need to be careful; they're looking for you", she asserted.

"Police?" I asked, feigning indifference.

'Please not them.'

'Yet if not police...'

'Who?'

"No, not the police. Some Turks my brother got himself involved with." All at once, being Dan descended on me, intrigued and surprised by these developments, the character assumed control with slick adroitness.

"Turks?"

"They killed him where you'd met up. It's one of his hideouts. They know you were involved somehow. They're Turkish mafia...or whatever they call themselves. They think you have his shipment, or the money he got for it."

"Shipment of what for God's sake?"

"Well not fucking gold bars, that's for sure!"

"Fucking hell."

"Too fucking right fucking hell!" Raw emotion came through the static of the CB set. Val had never sounded this way. But then she'd never had her brother killed before. "It's not safe to talk on here. They're serious. I need to speak to you again soon, when I know more." Val's uncharacteristic doubtful tones troubled me.

"When?"

"I don't know, but soon. Next day or two, ok?"

"Yeah, what time?"

"I don't fucking know. Be on here around this time tomorrow, if not sooner." Click. The set went dead. Val had switched off, not just ended the transmission. Cut the power to her rig completely.

We spoke again the following evening. Val being most concerned about the Turkish types looking for me. She went on to explain that they were after a substantial sum of money. Payment for a large shipment of narcotics Sean had imported and been in the process of distributing around the country.

These people had become convinced I had either the money, the drugs, or both. They wanted me dead, I could tell that much, but not before recuperating their pride by recovering the money or the contraband.

They came after me. Or rather Dan. They came up empty, and wound-up dead.

A whole week passed before Val made contact, sounding desperate. Describing how the bastards had been to her place and caused some damage. To show they meant business. The worst of it was they had made threats, next time the damage would be done to *her.* Compelling me to encounter them.

I told Val to set up a meeting for the following week. Promising to return their money plus an extra three thousand for the inconvenience. The Turks agreed but demanded an extra five-thousand. Having expected this, I concurred. The meeting would be between myself and two of them.

Doubtless more would be there, hiding close by, ready to swoop in. It wouldn't matter. They would not be expecting the trouble they were in for. My whole mindset shifted onto a war-footing. Taking them out became a crusade. Protecting Val from any form of retribution. Perhaps I sought redemption.

What to expect from these Turkish mobsters? Would they carry guns? I doubted it. Not in England. Not to deal with Dan, all by himself. Knives though, were a certainty. However, I reasoned either way, they wouldn't consider me a threat. Intending to overwhelm me. Good. Mobsters, gangsters, tough guys. Whoever they were, they were in for a nasty surprise. What choice did I have? Although this didn't feel like God's Wrath anymore. Just another raid in another war.

PART THREE

MY WAR

This anticipated, dreadful confrontation compelled my honed military senses to take control. The situation demanded professionalism. Being a soldier had been my first and only profession. The immediate objective would be to acquire a decent handgun. The *Fabrique Nationale* factory in Belgium supplied a brand-new, Mk I lightweight, Browning Hi-Power 9mm pistol. Via a military connection from years prior now residing in Lille. A former member of the French Foreign Legion who went by the name of Zoltan. We'd done mercenary work together in West Africa. A brilliant soldier, only the loss of a foot had kept him from further action.

At least a decade older than myself, he'd found and married a wife from the little French border town and built a life out there. They owned a few hotels and a nightclub in the town. No-one ever seemed to know from whence he'd originated but Zoltan's ability to speak Flemish as well as French served me well in this present purpose. I knew for a fact he spoke Hungarian but rumours had him of French heritage although born and raised somewhere in The Balkans. Having saved my life on numerous occasions a trust had developed between us in the field of battle that remained ever since.

I'd gotten him out when he lost his foot. Crushed by falling masonry as we lay exchanging fire with insurgent guerrillas. Zoltan had barely acknowledged the injury, keeping the enemy pinned down as we'd executed our withdrawal. Later that day he told me to chop off his foot as it could not be saved. With strong South African gin in his gut, cattle-rope clamped between teeth and grim acceptance on his visage, Zoltan cursed spittle through his bite until I brought a hatchet down on his ankle. His foot fell off the block as blood soaked into it. Zoltan had writhed, clutching at his fresh stump. I left the hatchet buried in the block.

———◆———

This renown Browning pistol came with a thirteen-cartridge magazine. Lucky number, maybe. Unlucky for someone. The weapon was familiar to me from my service days. The British military used them, as did most of the Commonwealth countries of that time. However, although Zoltan's contact supplied me with a brand-new weapon, it had not recently come off the production line at *Fabrique Nationale*. Rather it came from an avid enthusiast. A former employee of the famed Belgian small-arms factory, who had a collection of his own, for sale only to specialists. Zoltan's speciality happened to be guns. The acquiring and supplying of them. As an aside to his legal business activities.

Only manufactured during the 1950's, the Mark I Lightweight variant had been designed for use by Paratroops and thus constructed of a lighter alloy. Perfect for my intentions. Zoltan had recommended the model to me when we'd spoken on the 'phone, a few days before my flight over. Figuring the lighter weight would off-set my lack of practice. Also, I'd carried and used a regular model Browning for months at a time during my service days. It seemed prudent to use a lighter version of the potent weapon, rather than a different pistol altogether. I knew this gun would do my work. Thirteen nine-millimetre, eight-point-three gramme bullets. With another clip ready in my pocket, twenty-six slugs to kill at least two of these dangerous Turkish mobsters.

I met Zoltan at his popular club in Lille, on Rue Nicolas Leblanc. The place had a modern feel to it. Colourful bands created an avant-garde atmosphere, catalysed by lava lamps and the pervading aroma of Patchouli oil and Marijuana joints. Turning up at seven I had dinner sat in a small booth whilst listening to a succession of performers. I smiled at people but my knowledge of French being limited, remained apart from the general *joy de vie*.

The food all seemed a bit mysterious. So, a simple platter of local breads and cheeses sufficed. Washed down with a glass of fine Burgundy. This kept my appetite at bay until able to return to my chartered aircraft at the Aeroport de Lille-Lesquin and get back to England the following morning. The pilot and owner of the Cessna I'd chartered awaited me there.

A tall waitress came over. In a beautiful, accented voice, she asked; "If you are ready now you can follow me Monsieur Daniels?" With a nod I got up as she turned and led the way, her figure swaying with appealing mesmerism. Dark locks swung in time with broody hips. Leading me through a staff door into a private area. Several corridors led off to different parts of the building. We went along one of these. Although, internally, my attention had shrunk right down to the present moment. Shared between this alluring woman and myself. Sultry stilettos clacked and scraped on hard stone slabs. She cleared her throat. An intense feeling of intimacy and spontaneity exploded into my awareness. Long seconds passed, pervaded with seductive thoughts dancing between us. The molecules of the air seemed to thicken. A quiet crackle of suppressed lust haunted our short journey. From her to me, or me to her, I could not tell. Then, without further sound or pause, this bombshell of a French mademoiselle turned right and unlocked another door. Standing aside and holding it open for me to pass through. Our eyes met but her expression gave nothing away. Hadn't she felt it too? Hadn't she caused it? Perhaps my imagination had run ahead of me. Unusual.

Smiling, hoping I appeared as cool as she did, I ducked beneath her left arm. Whilst doing so the waitress scraped the fingernails of her free hand down the back of my neck with a surprising depth of focused passion. Squeezing her waist with one hand in acknowledgement yet still moving, I went into the doorway. Our little connection, having been so briefly announced and confirmed, could wait until later.

———⊰◆⊱———

The opening led into a small room with a plain, rectangular table, several chairs, storage boxes and Zoltan. Hairy and swarthy as ever. No male-pattern baldness in his pirate genes. Cigar chomped firmly between teeth. Propping himself half-up onto his one leg to welcome me. The stump of the other resting on a cushion in his seat. I leaned over to grasp his hand, of course he pulled me close for a hug and mutual shoulder slap.

"Here you are at last! Good to see you my friend! Here, sit down, I have brandy for you. Did you eat?" He said whilst bumping back into a more relaxed position.

"I did, thank you. I could do with a brandy, good choice."

"Of course, Sam! Of course! Don't I know you so well?" Zoltan's enthusiasm tended to bastardise his English even more than he already spoke it. Cigar smoke overlaid the aroma of the brandy when I sniffed it. The taste overcame all else though. Magnificent.

"Magnifique!" My exclamation bursting from a warmed throat with evident glee.

"Is it not so?" He asked in that back-to-front manner deemed necessary in French. I smiled, nodding my appreciation. The room hardly extended beyond the table being used as a desk. Containing a clutter of stationary and an ancient typewriter. Low bass tones throbbed and thrummed through the walls and woodwork. The high pitch crackle of a badly tuned radio popped and whistled from the grey windowsill. Drapes coloured an unattractive orange and brown concealed the window. My old friend gestured to a wicker kitchen chair to my right. We sat at angles to each other, across one corner of the table.

"I assume we can talk openly in here?" My question being rhetorical, a reply would be superfluous. Instead, Zoltan gave me a look and shrugged. Then reached beneath his own chair and brought out the Browning's case.

"We don't have to talk at all if you don't want to old friend, discretion is all part of the service, no?" He leaned back puffing on his cigar, gazing into my eyes from beneath bushy, dark eyebrows.

Zoltan knew me well enough. He knew I could take care of myself without the need of such a specialist weapon. Although why I needed it, he did not know. I leaned forward, maintaining his gaze. He pushed the gun-case towards me with his single Cuban-heeled boot. Picking it up and smiling back at him, a sudden grin spread across my face. Not a shred of hostility existed between us. A feeling we both knew so well but hadn't shared together for over a decade. This sensation grew as the gun passed between us. Rising into our awareness like a friendly, warm abode. It enveloped the room. Pervading the atmosphere and destroying all need for awkwardness. We both realised in that moment he would be the one and only person I could share this particular secret with.

"Intrigued?" I asked.

"Oh, I see the mischief in your eyes you know! You would love to tell me why you need this pistol, Samuel!" He chided in an exaggerated whisper. "You cannot get past old Zoltan, Sergeant de la legion!" He exclaimed. Accenting his words with a sharp salute which knocked the cigar from his mouth. His antics had the pair of us laughing like old schoolboys. I hadn't felt so free in years.

"I have to shoot some bad guys Zoltan. For a female acquaintance. To clear up a mess I've made."

"Okay, now we're talking", he said. Dropping the smile in an instant. "Bad guys, eh?" He re-lit the fading cigar. Then nodded, raising those bushy brows at me. "Go on."

"Well, that's it."

"Wha? Ques que ce?!" He blasted, rocking in his seat. Then, after an exaggerated and overt raising of his vivacious eyebrows, Zoltan spoke calmer; "You know Sam, you always infuriated me. Mr mystery man still today, eh?" He winked. Then, exploding back into animation with - "Who are they? These bad guys then? You tell me now." I sighed, then took a large swig of the brandy.

"All I know is they are some sort of gangsters. You know, mobsters. I killed someone who owes them money for heroin. They think I have their money, their narcotics, or both. An arrangement has been made where I'll pay them back in full, plus an extra five grand for their inconvenience."

"In exchange for what? Your life?" Zoltan's eyebrows almost connected with inquiry.

"No. Hers."

"Ah, oui. I see. Your female 'acquaintance', non?"

"Yes. They have threatened her."

"And the man you killed is their friend, yes?"

"No. He was her brother."

"What?!" Zoltan sat bolt upright with surprise. "This does not sound like you Sam." He exclaimed, shaking his head. "But it does sound like a bad mess." Shaking his head again in disbelief, before sipping on his Cognac. "And *you* made this mess?" He asked. His expressions, both physical and aural, were full of incredulity. Reminding me of just how out of control my hidden savagery had become. Zoltan's warrior-wisdom read my inner contemplations. With a much lower tone, he shifted the emphasis to me. Asking with great care; "Part of you still needs the excitement, yes?" He didn't embarrass me by pausing for a reply. "Well, we all have our cross to bear, no?"

"Indeed we do Zoltan. We certainly do." I opened the case and took the gun out, hefting it from hand to hand, holding it up to the light to inspect the details of its design. What a glorious contrivance of a pistol. Holding it rewarded me with inordinate sensations of ability and purpose. The lighter weight clearly apparent, despite not having held a handgun for a number of years at that moment.

The grip, an elementary knurled effect formed into the alloy handle. No extra wood or comfortable ergonomics for this model. Yet, within seconds the metal felt warm in my hand. Warm and light, but solid. Such a well-crafted device, built for death alone. A beautiful implement. Perfect.

"Feel good? You like it? Zoltan's words broke my reverie.

"It's just the job, brilliant, perfect. Thanks Zoltan. Great recommendation. Do you have the extra clip?"

"I have two. One is a gift. In case you need it."

"I won't."

"But you don't know that. Do you even know how many of these people there are?"

"Two are coming to meet me. I expect there'll be more."

"Of course there will be more Sam. But you need to know none will be left who can still harm your friend. You need to get them all to come to meet you." He shuffled in his chair, folded his stump across his good leg and proceeded to itch at it. "You seem sure there aren't too many of them."

"There may well be Zoltan. But if there are and I get killed, my friend shall live."

"You cannot be sure of that. And you don't intend on getting yourself killed. Think about your friend. You need to be sure, monsieur." Leaning back in the chair and sipping at my glass, our eyes locked. He was intrigued alright. Deciding to indulge his direction of inquiry, I asked;

"You're right. What do you suggest?"

"Well, you know the drill Sam. Gather intelligence on the enemy, basic military strategy. What do you know about these people? Are they a big, well organised gang?"

"I know they're Turks. Turkish mafia, if you like. I doubt there's more than a car full of them in England, but they could have associates over there."

"Ok, forget about associates. Only the proper guys will come for you." Zoltan paused, puffed on his stogie, before inhaling and then letting out a long sigh. He looked up at me, in a fatherly way he had only shown on rare, private occasions whilst soldiering together. Holding the look until he registered my recognition of it. Then he stared to one side, eyes vacant, not seeing the room we sat in, as his mind pondering some issue of the ethereal kind, before looking back at me. "Now that I know this, my eyes see your situation differently. At first, I thought you meant a gang from England. That could be complex. This, you have offered them a promise, a compromise. Now you must make them a threat, you understand?"

"No. Why threaten them?"

"Why? To make sure they all come to meet you, of course! Turks are proud and prickly. Use this to your advantage."

"By threatening them? I'm not getting it." Zoltan gave me an exasperated look.

"But this will only be a minor threat, Samuel. A *petité* assertion, if you will. Okay, not so much a threat as a show of defiance. A lack of fear. That will be enough to dent their pride. They will want to intimidate you."

"Yes, but I'm expecting them to come at me anyway. They were never going to be happy just to get paid off."

"But you need to be sure my friend! Please, do this my way. I know how these people think. They will all want to be right there, heckling and staring. Only a carful? Four or five at the most you say?" He sat up straight and raised his chin at me with Gallic histrionics, inviting a response. I nodded, grave determination blazing from my eyes. "Then you should have no problems, no surprises. Not if you are fast", he asserted.

"I don't intend on negotiating, I'll have the cash with me, to distract them. Once they look at it…"

"Which they will." Zoltan pointed out, tapping the polished wooden armrest of his chair hard with his fingertips. This knocking sound woke a small dog up which had remained unnoticed by me until that instant. Its sudden, loud bark made me jump, heart skipping a beat. Zoltan laughed at my reaction, then shouted at the dog in French. Sounds of the dog growling and grumbling emanated from behind him somewhere, yet I never saw the thing.

"Which they will", Zoltan repeated, this time raising a finger with a knowing look.

"And then they'll be dead men." I envisaged, concluding the scenario. "Sound good?"

"Yes Sam, it does." He finished his Cognac with a flourish, wiping his moustache with the back of his hand. "Bon. Good. Maintenant, do you need anything else?" The alcohol expanding his propensity to mix languages.

"For the gun? No, everything's here. Except the holster."

"Ah, oui. The one for your shoulder? Like the FBI guys on the movies, non?" His hand formed the shape of a gun whilst enacting the motions of pulling a pistol from inside his jacket. This brought a rare chuckle from me.

"Yeah, that's it. You ever worn one?"

"Me? No, no." he scratched his beard, thinking. "Not my style. Is it not bulky beneath your arm?"

"Not sure, not worn one myself. Apparently, it does feel strange at first, but the draw is supposed to be quick."

"And a surprise for your bad guys!" Zoltan blurted, guffawing and rocking back and forth. Creating a symphony of rhythmic squealing from his chair.

"Absolutely. They won't know what hit them."

"But remember Sam", he pointed, voice lowering in earnestness, "do it swift, do it good …" He left the sentence hanging, looking right into me. Waiting.

"Do it right." I said, finishing his little mantra. The mantra he'd taught me years prior, out in Africa.

"That's right Mon Ami", he smiled. "Look behind you, the holster is hanging from the coat hook up there on that wall. I'm afraid it isn't made for this specific pistol, but you will see it is the correct size." I turned and looked up, eyes straining in the under-lit room. The leather of the holster, coloured light brown, stood bright against the gloom of the wall behind it. Having to stand to grab it, I then pulled the straps over my left arm. The aromatic new leather stiff and unyielding. Steel buckles were adjusted until achieving a snug fit. The Browning bulging, albeit comfortable, once in the holster. A further adjustment of the harness allowed for this mass of specialised alloy to fit beneath my suit jacket incognito.

"How does it feel now? Is it good?"

"Hmm, yeah. Not bad." Zoltan gestured for me to step towards him as he spoke. When close enough he began to pat at my jacket around the gun.

"The barrel is a little long for the holster, but not by much. Nothing to worry about. Try drawing it out." Before my hand had moved, he interjected; "With your finger on the trigger, well, on the guard at least."

"Ok." Getting my hand around the grip beneath my jacket proved a little awkward at first. Not like the movies.

"Slowly", he advised. With deliberateness, I practised getting a hold of the gun under my jacket. However, when drawn, the pistol dragged on the leather, pulling the holster with it. Further adjustments were necessary. Encouraged by Zoltan, within quarter of an hour these issues were ironed out. He looked at me, head tilted to one side, as if in consideration. His question felt loaded, but I could not figure his angle.

"So old friend, have you any idea what you are going to do once all the bad guy Turks are dead?"

"What do you mean? I don't intend on burying them Zoltan, if that's what you mean. They'll stay wherever they lay."

"They do not concern me. But what about your friend, your female acquaintance? Will she remain safe? How do you know more of these people will not come? They could already be in England, in London, Bristol, anywhere. Have you not thought about this?"

"I'll kill them and make sure she gets the money."

"Make sure? Can you not give her the money yourself? Aren't you going to kill these guys for her?"

"She knows nothing about me killing anyone and I intend to keep it that way. She has no need to know."

"Ah. She thinks they killed her brother."

"Correct, though God knows why. I went to meet her brother, to sell him some gold bullion. At least that's the story I made up. It was all a ploy to get him alone. I'd been seeing her for a while, good friends, good company, you know." I paused to swallow some more brandy; aware I was telling him far more than I'd ever intended. "Anyway, one day he just walked in. She'd never mentioned any brother. Right from the off, he acted like a right bastard, you know?" Zoltan nodded.

"You took an instant dislike then?"

"Dislike? More like detest! He made it easy enough. He was putting pressure on her. Threatened me, made it clear he didn't want me around. Things went quiet and he never showed up whenever I was at her place, but he kept leaning on her. I set-up the whole gold bullion scenario in order to get a chance at him."

"Oh yeah? How did that go?"

"He fell for it. We met up, I killed him."

"But no gun?"

"No need."

"I suppose not. But now, you need the gun. These bad guys outnumber you."

"That doesn't matter. It will make them confident. I do expect them to have knives though."

"You better believe it. Big knives. Bloody Magnum, Scimitars!" He waved an arm about his head as though brandishing one of the infamous Turkish cavalry swords. We laughed and the dog barked his complaint at Zoltan's chair rocking and knocking about. "You better believe it", he muttered again, much quieter. Then he stared at the table top, as though staring into space. Deep in thought. Not wishing to interrupt his reverie, I sat still and kept quiet. His brown eyes blinked and he looked at me with a new look on his face; "Maybe I can help, Sam. After all, why work alone? No, don't look at me that way. I do not mean myself, though - Mon Dieu! How I would love to be able to. No. But, you know old Zoltan…I have many connections across France, Belgium, most of Europe in fact." He babbled, not giving me a chance to reply. Because he knew I'd refuse the offer. Which I did. His efforts were heartfelt though, that much was obvious. We didn't mention my intentions again. Instead, once I'd handed him the kilo bar of Swiss gold bullion we'd agreed as price for acquiring the gun and holster, we spent several hours reminiscing and giving toasts to old friends and enemies alike.

Afterwards, I found the waitress. We didn't even speak, not properly. We didn't have to. Only exchanging pleasantries and names, hers being Odette. We were led by Zoltan's wife Emmanuelle up several flights of stairs to a room she had made up. She smiled at the pair of us, as if we were a honeymooning couple and this was her hotel. The remainder of the night full of passionate lovemaking, although upon awakening in the daylight I discovered Odette had gone. Placing my hands behind my head, I looked over at the gun-case sitting on the dresser. No worries. All is good. Time to get back to The Front.

THE PROFESSIONAL

O ne question perplexed me: - "If Zoltan had told me what had really been on his mind that night, would I still have gone about my business and gunned down those Turks?" It still does. This job was carried out with callous efficacy. Basic, simple. Far easier an affair than any of my chosen Targets ever were.

Through Val, arrangements to meet were agreed. At my chosen time and location. Five Turks showed-up. A car-full, as discussed with Zoltan. Five minutes later, five warm corpses lay on cold tarmac. No need to even reload. As tough as they were, they had no chance. Going into shock upon seeing my gun drawn and aimed at them. One of the five made an effort, coming close to chopping my hand off with his savage blade. Yet to no avail. They lay dead at my feet within minutes of meeting me. Easy work for a pro. Val however, proved to be far more difficult to deal with.

The gold. One factor which had escaped my mind. Not Val's though. Not at all. Those bright bars still glistened in her thoughts. Deceiving me, the great deceiver, into believing she thought the Turks had killed her brother.

The Turks had turned up in a large four-door Mercedes. All of them big, swarthy men in short, black leather jackets. Dressed to intimidate. Standing shoulder to shoulder, forming a wall, once they'd all exited the Merc. I played my part well. Acting as if chagrined, dubious and unsure of the outcome. Exactly what they wanted. For a minute or so. Buying time to ascertain there were no other vehicles present. Easy enough as we were on an unused airstrip. Wide open and spacious. Nothing but Wood Pigeons and Jackdaws pecking for worms in the turf for as far as my eyes could see. Time for action.

Before any of them spoke asking; - "Would you mind opening the boot of your car?" Whilst indicating with gestures to elucidate, gaining the initiative. At first, they looked confused but I held the hold-all with the cash up and their leader seemed to understand and spoke to one who turned and went towards the rear of their car. The leader admonished another of his henchmen, who'd cursed at me and protested with unfamiliar words at my initial signals, although his gestures and meaning had shone clear. Opening the hold-all to show off the cash, I took a five-grand wad and threw it towards the angry henchman, even surlier now, having just been put in his place. He caught it and seemed appeased, holding it out before him for the others to see. The cash in the hold-all caught all of their attention once I'd covered the few yards between us. Only for a second or so. Holding it towards them in my left hand, watching intently for the split-second they all looked down at the money. Just a heartbeat or two, yet time enough for me to draw the Browning and start shooting. They hardly even reacted. Apart from the one who'd been sent to open the boot of their car. He pulled a meat-cleaver from somewhere whilst I shot his friends down. From peripheral vision he took a couple of huge bounds towards me. With a mixture of ferocity and terror carved into swarthy features he swung the heavy steel blade at my gun hand. The last three bullets stopped him dead. Tearing holes right through his chest and out his back, he came so close. Despite this excitement, I vacated the scene breathing slow, with a steady pulse and dry hands.

Now my plans became vague. Wanting to drop the money off at Val's place, but in her absence, uncomfortable with the idea of meeting her in person ever again. Reasoning this reticence came from killing her brother. Ensuing occurrences however proved my instincts were warning me Val had already seen through my lies.

SWORN

A few hours after the shooting I drove to Val's. Debating all the while to myself. In the end, something other than logic or reason took me there. Certainly not instinct. Every sense in me prickled. Ruling out CB or any other means of attempting contact. With Sean and the Turks gone there would be no danger at Val's place. But facing her. Being Dan. Having to play my part in that corrupted, redundant script, dismayed me. Perhaps needing to console her, convincing her she was now safe. Despite being the single most dangerous person she ever knew.

The place turned out to be empty and quiet. No sign of Val's car or noise from her dogs. I checked around her narrowboat. There were obvious indicators she had been there that morning. Her hens were fed and hot ashes from the onboard coal-stove, held in an iron bin on the canal-side, still held a little warmth. Looking around the Lock-keepers cottage gave the same story, no one at home but signs of recent activity. Peering through the windows and mooching around her doors got me nowhere. Albeit I didn't mind. This was perfect. I'd leave the cash hidden in a sack beneath the bench of one of her glasshouses. Her favourite one.

However, during the process, sounds of Val's car approaching stopped me in my tracks. Frozen to the spot. Standing in the glasshouse with the hold-all under my arm like a statue. For once in my life at a loss as to what to do. Knowing Val must have seen my car. The sound of tyres crunching onto the driveway grew closer. Thoughts of having to become Dan again clenched my heart. My throat tightened. I made spit and swallowed hard, breathing slow.

A cold sweat erupted from the back of my head, drips forming on my hair-ends. Gritty, hard reality pounded at my awareness in vain. Panic befuddled my senses, sending me blundering into a very difficult situation. After placing the hold-all beneath one of the benches and pushing some loose sacking and empty seed-trays above to obscure it from view, I walked towards the sliding doors.

Val's car rolled around the side of the house. Coming to a stop at the edge of the concreted yard, close to a lawn that acted as a garden for her boat. Sliding the doors apart, I stood in the opening with my right hand holding one door by the high corner. The afternoon had become overcast, bringing a gloom to the area, so switching on the glasshouse lights to help Val find me seemed pertinent.

"That you Dan?" She called a few moments later, whilst climbing from the car. Voice friendly, although her gaze not being directed towards me. Instead dealing with her dogs, guiding them towards the boat. Of course, they came running over to me first before she called them back.

"Yeah, saw you weren't around so I thought I'd wait in here. Knew you probably wouldn't be gone too long." I called back over to her, lying as Dan, as ever. Val remained focused on her dogs, calling each by name until they left my petting and ran back to her. Despite her failure to respond to my answer, at the time, this fact escaped my notice. Attempting to play the role clogged my synapses. I'd never had to hide my emotions as Dan prior to this moment. Always having the comfort of being able to be natural for the most part. This felt quite singular.

"You been waiting here very long?" She called, now walking away with the dogs towards the narrowboat.

"Not really Val, got here about fifteen minutes ago." Being Dan slid over me like a velvet lined glove.

'Glad to hear it. You want to wait there a minute while I sort these dogs out? I won't be long." Val disappeared onto her narrowboat without waiting for me to reply. She seemed to be in a good mood so I felt it best to do as she asked. It also gave me time to consider my options. Deciding to tell her the Turks had been paid and were no longer a threat to her. She did not need to know they were dead. My earlier anticipation melted away. Ensuring Val did not discover the cash before I left. To this end I propped a stool against the bench in front of the hold-all, then sat upon it waiting.

The little gate to the houseboat clinked shut indicating Val had finished and now walked over towards the glasshouse. As she passed the windows on her way to the door at the far end, she spoke to me, still with only a glance my way though, I noted.

"All done then Dan? Did it go well?" Her tone still light and friendly. Albeit her form remained obscured by plants up against the glass. Then the quickening of Val's steps as she got closer to the door caught my attention. Something about the charade I played vexed my senses. Reducing honed perceptions to insipidness. Thinking about being Dan and producing convincing lies clouded my brain to what really went on around me. Yet even at this rather unconscious level of operating, an incongruity about Val's words and actions stung gently at my dulled instincts.

"Did you sell that gold to pay off the Turks then Dan?" Her question put me off. The gold being the last thing occupying my thoughts at that precise moment. Those shining, seductive bars, had not crossed my mind since placing them in my safe deposit box at Coutts on The Strand within a few days of killing Sean.

"Eh? Oh, yeah. Course I did Val, where'd ya think I got the money to pay them from?"

"That's what I thought. Did you get a good price for it in the end then?" By this point, Val had reached the far end of the footpath but instead of turning left towards the sliding door she crossed the driveway and went towards the house. Without waiting for my reply, she said; "Hang on there Dan I need to get something." Before being able to form a reasonable response, she'd walked briskly to the front door of the cottage, unlocked it and stepped inside.

Could I really be Dan, one last time? It felt impossible. I'd rather have run naked back to London. Those brief moments alone, waiting among Val's plants, tormented me with doubt and indecision. In itself an unnerving, unfamiliar feeling. What did Val expect of Dan at this point? Hoping it would not be intimacy. Knowing this would be insufferable. Being so cold-hearted stood beyond my capabilities. Not to mention sensibilities. Having torn the face off her brother. And knowing nothing of his funeral, or her grief. Nothing. Also, Val's affability since discovering me at her home so soon after meeting the Turks seemed inapt. Forced even.

The front door of the cottage slammed shut. The little wooden stool scraped across the concrete floor as I stood up to greet her. Val's silhouette flickered across the window panes as she approached. Wishing to put space between myself and the hold-all I moved down the centre towards the door. Twenty-five thousand pounds cash sat in that bag. Val would find it. She'd want to move the stool before watering the plants, which would reveal the bag.

"No need to get up Dan, I've got just what you need right here!" Val's voice rose to a crescendo. Delivered as she swung into my view. Filling the doorway, shotgun clasped in her slender hands, pointed at the floor. She went to raise the gun and shoot me in the heart, I think. Either that or the head. Instead, the gun went off as she jerked it upwards, sending instant pain searing through my brain. The noise tore my left eardrum apart, the concussion contained by the glass and brickwork. A blinding, burning sting came to my awareness. Val loomed. Too large. Why was she so tall now? Then lucidity returned, if not my senses. I was on the floor. Shot. My left hand wet with the flow of blood it aimlessly attempted to stem. Shock hit me again. Causing me to wince and cry out. A red glow enveloped my senses. An excruciating numbness overcame me. A burning steam of opium vapours swathed my perceptions, at once scolding and removing me from the pain. But the sound of a voice brought me back to attention. My own voice. Screaming in the distance. Calling out for my mother. Pain raked through me. Val had shot me twice. Both barrels, from barely ten yards away. Pain meant I still lived. Yet how?

"You can scream all you like, no one's going to hear you. Go on. Scream for your mother. Scream for your father, your sister, your brother. It won't make any fucking difference. *Dan.*"

Val spat the name with unadulterated vehemence. Making it obvious it no longer meant anything to her. Yet her words also brought me round somewhat. From the haze and delirium of shock and pain. Bloody wetness oozed beneath me and into my trousers from serious wounds on my left side.

"Val, please" My voice croaked, throat dry, limbs uncontrolled, spasmodic, quivering with adrenaline. Helpless.

"Val. That's right. That's *my* name. But what's *your* name then, eh? Because I certainly know it's not fucking Dan!" Delivering a vicious kick to my kidney with the last syllable, she then followed through by smacking me in the head with the stock of the shotgun. The blows kept coming.

Splash. Cold water struck my face. The coolness felt good. And again. This time with more force. Droplets got up my nose and a bout of racking coughs exploded from me. Snot, blood and spittle flew out, projected with velocity across the cold concrete floor. Consciousness delivered pain. Searing, stinging, and burning sensations ran up and down the skin of my whole left side, but the open wounds were torture. As though my raw flesh had been doused with vinegar. I sucked air in through clenched teeth, wincing and grimacing with every motion.

"Aww, did you sleep well?' Val mocked, throwing another pan of cold water into my spluttering face. Rolling, coughing, squelching in a puddle of blood and water. Additional pain from fresh lumps on my skull stabbed through all else to announce their recent creation with alacrity. "What you got to say for yourself now then Danny boy? Not saying much now, are we, eh? No. Not very much at all. Well, you get yourself comfortable and when you've thought about what you need to tell me then let me know because I'm all ears, Mister."

"Alright Val, I'll tell you. Least I can do."

"Too fucking right it is! This is the real you talking now, isn't it? Whoever the fuck you are. That's the most real thing you've ever said to me, do you know that? All those nights we spent together. All those good times. I really liked being with you, ya know. It was obvious you were hiding something but I never dreamt you could ever hurt me. I think the "*least you can do*" is tell me why you fucking killed my brother, before I kill you."

"I've killed before Val, many times. No, you're right, my name is not Dan." These words took some saying. However, I did manage to roll over onto my right side and prop myself up on one elbow. I padded around the wounds on my left side, trying to ascertain the extent of the damage. Plenty of blood flowed out from several large gashes, but there weren't the chunks of tissue missing the pain indicated. The damage seemed to be evenly spread between my left armpit and knee, with my waist and thigh being most hurt. It looked more like the spread of a sawn-off shotgun. Despite the screeching pain, curiosity tugged at my thoughts.

"Really? Is that right?" Val asked with a sarcastic tone and expression. Then; - "How about telling me something I don't already fucking know?" Her vehemence and hatred were profound. I knew any shadow of my former pretence would get me killed as quick as it would take Val to pull the trigger.

"I'll tell you anything you want but I need to stop this bleeding soon."

"No, you don't."

"Oh, I'm gonna die anyway, is that it? But then you'd never know, would you?" Pain stung into my chest as it expanded with the effort of speaking. My words rasping out in slow whispers. Val remained unmoved. Studying me. When she seemed satisfied my injuries were enough to keep me immobile, she took out a pack of her favourite variety of John Player Special cigarettes and lit one between her teeth. All the while the shotgun hung from the crook of her left arm.

"Never know what?" She asked.

"What d'ya think? Why I killed Sean. Isn't that what this is about? Otherwise, I'd be dead already. If you want to know, I need to tell you before I lose too much blood."

"So, fucking well tell me then! You could have told me by now! Listen, you won't fucking bleed to death. The cartridges I shot you with were eighty percent rock salt. Stings, doesn't it? Part of me wanted to kill you outright but part of me wants you to suffer. Most of all though I want answers. Sean was a bastard, I know. I've known since we were kids something would happen to him. That he'd get himself in so much trouble he'd wind up dead. But you had no reason to kill him. And leave him to be eaten away by wild animals. There was hardly fuck all left of him by the time he were found! I don't know how or why you killed him and I don't want to know the how. But I do want you to tell me why. Now, stop whinging and fucking tell me, before I blow your fucking toes off and really give you something to cry about, you lying, deceiving bastard."

"Rock salt? You shot me with rock salt?"

"Yeah. Learnt it from dad. Take most of the shot out of the cartridges and replace with rock salt. I knew it wouldn't do you too much damage because I practised on sacks of potatoes yesterday. Enough but not too much. Not yet. But don't worry, it's loaded for real now. So don't fuck about. Now tell me."

"I never had a good reason for killing Sean though Val. That's just it. Everyone else I ever killed before was a right horrible bastard."

"What, are you some kind of hit man then?"

"Not the way you think. I worked for myself. No one paid me to kill anyone."

"So why did you kill them then? Who were they?"

"Like I said, horrible types with blood on their hands. I did it because I could. Because I like it. I used to be a soldier. I was involved in lots of action, out in Africa. As a mercenary. My own businesses and investments paid for my way of life."

"Your way of life? That's one fucking way to put it I suppose."

"Well, yeah. CB inspired me to create Dan. To meet new people, who knew nothing about me. I thought I could stop the killing by being someone else. It worked too. Until that Sunday Sean walked in on us, remember? It happened in here, right here where I'm bleeding now. This is where we were stood when he walked in through those doors behind you."

"Yeah, I remember. So what?"

"How did you know it was me and not the Turks who killed Sean?" Val stared at me, then drew long and hard on the cigarette, finishing it off. She threw the butt to the floor and stubbed it out. All whilst staring into my eyes.

"You're not as clever as you think, are you?" She asserted, a smirk at the corner of her mouth.

"What do you mean?"

"It was me that told the Turks about you, stupid! I sent them to take that money and cut you to pieces!" She stopped. Looking around, as if catching a scent. Then turned back to me, levelling the gun at my right knee. "By the way, where is that money? I know you kept most of it with you. One of those Turkish lads you shot this morning had a wad of fresh English cash in his hand. Did you bring it here with you? You must have. Were you trying to stash it here, for me?"

"That's right Val, I was. It's behind me here, under the bench, by the stool."

"Is it? Right behind you under the bench there?"

"Yes, I was hoping to get in and out without seeing you."

"And fuck off into the sunset? To never darken my doors ever again? Was that it?"

"Pretty much Val, yeah."

"How much is in there?"

"Twenty-five grand. I took the thirty-grand agreed to meet the Turks, to distract them as much as anything. After shooting them I left the cash in that one's hand because it didn't make much difference to me. I thought maybe whoever found them would keep it. Hardly even thought about it to be honest."

"Well, I found them, so I took it. Now you'd better get that bag and let me see if you're telling the truth or not. If you try anything, you won't even have time to regret it. Keep that in mind. I'm watching your every move."

"I can't move Val, it's too much."

"You'd better get it or shuffle your way out of the fucking way because I don't trust you. Now get a shift on before I lose my temper again." With a grimace, plenty of curses and spit frothing through gritted teeth as fresh pain ripped into me, I pushed myself back to the stool. This effort left me gasping and sobbing with pain. I had to stop and rest my head on the seat of the stool for a moment whilst catching my breath. Val refrained from rushing me, or goading me to go faster. She just left me to it. Once recovered, I pushed the stool out of the way, reached under, grabbed the hold-all, then leant back and threw it down the aisle towards Val. "Okay, now stay right as you are whilst I see what we've got here." Levelling the gun at me, she moved forward and took the hold-all by its handles, placing it onto the bench beside her after pushing a few plants aside to make space. "Well, well. You can tell the truth after all can't you?" She said after a quick look at the cash.

"Of course I can."

"But I still don't get it. Why would you bother leaving this money here for me? Was it guilt?"

"Maybe. But I thought you were afraid of the Turks, remember? You had me thinking they were putting you under a lot of pressure. As far as I was concerned you thought the Turks had killed Sean. They were never going to get that money. Once they were dead it seemed you had a right to it. Doesn't make that much difference to me."

"Thirty grand doesn't make much difference? Wow. How rich are you?"

"A lot wealthier than you think. Some of my better investments can return me twenty-five grand every quarter."

"So, you're telling me that there's a lot more where that came from?" She asked, gesturing towards the hold-all.

"Plenty."

"Thirty grand won't do it."

"Won't do what?" Val ignored my question. Instead, countering with one of her own.

"What did you do with the gold?" I could only stare at her. She lit another cigarette, dismissive of my response. Then went on. "You never found that much gold in any car. I bet you bought it, or already owned it, didn't you?"

"Yes. Your right. I bought it and used it to tempt Sean."

"Just to kill him." Her words soft, distant.

"Yes. To do that. I was out of control Val. Being Dan to stop my activities pushed it all beneath the surface.'

"All what? I don't get what you mean. You still haven't told me why you killed Sean.

"My urge to kill. That's what killed Sean. By giving it no outlet, all the while I pretended to be Dan, it lurked beneath the surface. But when Sean walked in on me the spell was broken and my murderous side took control again."

"As easy as that. You just decide to kill him because you didn't like him? What are you, some kind of maniac? You're not happy unless you kill someone?"

"No, not quite. I may be a maniac, yes, but Sean was different. He said himself you would only have peace over his dead body." I spat blood, clearing my mouth in order to speak. Val had belted me around the face, or kicked me when I passed out, as the insides of my cheeks were cut and swollen. "You know he would always have been trouble. He had his own plans for this place Val. That's the impression I got. And no, that is not reason enough to take a man's life. But the way Sean and I met, with me acting as Dan, the outcome was inevitable. Sean could sense I was hiding something, he was right not to trust me. His instincts were spot-on. He knew Dan was a fraud anyway."

"You talk as if Dan was someone else! Just because you used a different name doesn't mean it wasn't you!"

"No. It doesn't. I was out of control. You have every right to kill me. But I can't give you any more reason than I already have as to why I killed Sean. That's all there is to it. He was the way he was and I was pretending to be normal. I'm not."

"Fucking hell fire I won't argue with that. But I'm not going to shoot you again, not unless I need to. Your already fucked. If I don't get you some help before too long you won't live more than another forty-eight hours at most I reckon. Your life is in my hands now."

"If you're not going to shoot me, what do you want?"

"I ain't fucking said I want nothing yet 'ave I?" She raged. For all you know I could be planning on handing you over to the friends of those Turks you killed! To be tortured and buried alive!"

"But you're not. You know it makes no sense to kill me. Sooner or later, it will come back to you. I will be missed. My tracks will be re-traced. At the very least you will forever be looking over your shoulder, wondering when that knock at your door will come. I'm worth far more to you alive and a lot less trouble."

"The gold. I'll have that for a start. But how the fuck can we make this work? I'm not letting you out of my sight nor off my property until this deal is done."

"What do you want?"

"I need a guarantee that you won't come after me at a later date. You could turn up and shoot me dead as easy as you did those Turkish gangsters earlier. But I can't think for the life of me how you can guarantee that. All you ever did was lie to me, how am I supposed to believe a word you say? That's the problem we have here Mister."

"I don't kill women. Never have, never will. I'm not like that. But if you want some kind of reassurance, some insurance, I may be able to work something out. Something legal and binding. I won't come after you Val, I deserve this. Your right, my life is in your hands. I'll die here if you don't get me out or bring me help. I can't get very far at all by myself. I need time to think but if you let me, you could end up a lot better off than you are."

"Oh yeah and how is that?"

"I'll make you the owner of one of my businesses."

"I don't know how to run any business. What kind of business?"

"A haulage firm. It's perfect for you. The place runs itself, for the most part. You never know, you might improve it, make some changes for the better. Or if you prefer, I'll employ a general manager to ensure you turn a good profit. Which will be yours to reinvest in the company or do with as you please. Place makes around two hundred thousand profit each year, give or take. Take it. It's yours. That, the cash. All yours." By this point I'd managed to struggle up into a sitting position with my back against one of the aluminium legs of the benches.

"How? How are you going to do all this?" Val asked, her brow furrowing and head tilted in doubt.

"My secretary. She is in London but she'll have access to all the legal documentation for the business side of things, if you allow me to speak with her on the 'phone." I managed to gasp out.

"Your secretary? Are you fucking kidding me? I'm supposed to trust some bimbo strumpet you've got typing for you down in London, with all this shit? Think again mister, you'll have to do better than that. I'm not fucking joking." Val lifted the gun barrel and pointed it at me again to demonstrate her conviction.

"Neither am I!" The words hissed through gritted teeth hard with the pain propelling them like steam from a kettle. "She is a lot more than a secretary. But that's what she is. All you need to know is she can and will do as we ask."

"What will you tell her?"

"I don't know just yet. Don't want to alarm her, but need her to know how urgent the situation is. This could be tricky but I think I can pull it off."

"You think? You'd better be fucking sure Mister, or no deal. I'll let you die here and take my chances with the law if I have to, remember that." She rested the gun beside her on an open stretch of the bench before taking out and lighting another cigarette. After inhaling a few times, mulling it over whilst I sat there bleeding, Val picked up the shotgun and walked backwards down the aisle towards the doorway, cigarette hanging from her mouth. "You'll have to drag yourself out of there then, if you would like to use the 'phone."

"All the way into the cottage?"

"Well, I won't be fucking helping you!" Her shout reverberated around the glass walls and ceiling, angry words tumbling into a cold, dark silence. Squelching around in the patch of blood and water gave no clue as to how much blood had oozed from my wounds. My best guess being half a pint. The bleeding had slowed or even stopped on the lesser scratches and tears in my flesh, but deep wounds kept pushing fresh blood out. Strength ebbed from me each minute as much as blood did. Val scared me. She was serious. Albeit pragmatic. Her pragmatism kept me alive, as long as I could do as she asked. The thought of scraping myself along the aisle of the glasshouse, out across the driveway to her front door and into the hallway where the telephone sat on its little table filled me with despair. I could hardly sit up, was in shock and weakening fast. The absolute depths of my resolve and determination would have to be plundered for me to make it to Val's telephone. She stood in the doorway, waiting for me to make an effort.

"Alright, I'll do it." My words came out even weaker than expected. Followed by a rasping cough which left me grimacing once more as the motion caused fresh waves of pain to erupt from my wounds. Val said nothing, turned and walked towards the cottage, leaving the sliding doors open. The rhythmic sound of footsteps across the loose asphalt ground of the driveway gave way to the familiar noise of the front door to the cottage being opened. It did not close. I sat there a while. The rapidity of events on that day overwhelming my senses. A long sigh left my mouth, chest rising and falling in resignation of my dire predicament. How had it come to this? Moments, or minutes passed. It is impossible to say which. My breathing slowed and became regular. Leaning against the aluminium leg of the bench felt good. A lot had happened. Closed eyes enjoyed the peace of dimness. The quiet beckoning my mind into silence. Fatigue drew on my consciousness, pulling it down into the restful gloom of slumber. Drifting me off into sweet oblivion.

At once my right leg flopped sideways to the floor, jolting me awake. This would not do. Movement became imperative. The effects of adrenaline were wearing off. Tiredness would overcome me with ease if I didn't force myself along the aisle. I looked at the distance. Only about thirty feet to the doors. It seemed much farther. With my head towards the entrance, I lay on my right side. Using the legs of one bench to push against with my feet whilst pulling on the next pair with my hands, I managed to progress towards the sliding doors. Stretching and pulling myself caused agony, but proved less difficult than anticipated once into a rhythm. Pain tormented me anyway. Might as well use what strength remained to do everything possible to survive.

'Get to Val's 'phone. Call Mary.'
'Then, what? Tell her what exactly?'
'Tell her you are hurt first. Then tell her about Val.'
'When will I receive the medical attention I need?
'When Mary has satisfied Val's demands.'
'Will Mary even be in to answer the 'phone?'
'That depends.'
'On what?'
'Whatever time it is. Whatever day it is.'

'Do you remember?'
'Do you?'
'Will Val wait for Mary to do whatever she has to do?'
'What do you think?'

Questions were cast aside as the enormous effort took over my entire concentration. The long benches ended a yard or so from the doorway, causing me to lie full stretch in order to manoeuvre myself out of the glasshouse altogether. Sat against the entrance outside under the broiling night sky I looked back to where I'd started. A trail of blood led back to the puddle by the overturned stool. The exertion had my heart pounding, fresh blood squirted from the worst of the gunshot wounds, now brushed and stung by the slightest breeze. With nothing to push or pull against outside I had a problem. The wall of the glasshouse gave me a boost into the middle of the asphalt but from there nothing stood between me and the porch. Without any sort of purchase all I could do was roll myself. This caused immense pain each time my left side went beneath me. Even more blood pushed out and I yelped in agony as sharp aches stabbed out from the gashes. Once within reach of the porch I pulled myself in, flopping in the open doorway, overcome with pain and exhaustion.

"Nearly there, looks like your gonna make it." Val's voice brought me back to awareness. I attempted to nod but just slumped further into the doorway. Val took the telephone from its position on the little table and placed it on the floor so I could use it. Still out of reach, I had to drag myself the last few feet right up to the 'phone. Val gave me several paper towels to wipe my hands and had placed sheets of newspaper on the tiled floor of her hallway in anticipation of the blood coming from me. Lifting the receiver, a prayer crossed my lips for Mary to save me. Dialling Mary's number had never been an issue prior, yet it seemed to take forever to make this call. Cold, clammy fingers, shaking, stumbling, struggled to find the correct positions, forcing me to start over and redial the whole number several times before getting it right. The line clicked into life, followed by the ringing tone bursting out from the earpiece. My heart leapt. Within seconds the receiver at the other end of the line was picked up. Mary's sweet voice brought tears of relief to my eyes.

"Hello?" She enquired, unsure who might be calling. Val stepped towards me and leaned in to hear better. She no longer had the shotgun. By this point there being no real need for it.

"Mary it's me." I croaked. Before I could say any more Mary's voice came back excited and also relieved.

"Sam! I knew you would call tonight! I've had the strangest feeling for the last, oh, nearly an hour now. I knew it! Listen we need to talk, I'm glad you rang because I've got a lot to tell you."

"I haven't got time for business matters now Mary. I need you to help me out."

"Of course, I'll get round to that. Right now though I need to tell you what's been happening here in London. I've got so much to tell you!"

"Mary, I love you with all my heart. But I need you to listen to me. I've been seriously hurt. I'm captive. I need to pay them off. Whatever I tell you, you must not go to the police at all. If you do, I'll die before they get here. Do you understand?" This time a pause answered my words. Now I'd gained her attention. I hadn't meant to tell Mary that I loved her. The words flew from my mouth as the emotion swept through me at the sound of her voice, facilitated by my heightened emotions of the situation and the desperate need for her to come and rescue me.

"No Sam, I don't understand. Not at all." Mary answered, failing to suppress the entirety of the surprise and delight in her voice. "But I will do as you say, exactly. Whatever it takes, I'm bringing you home with me from wherever you are right now."

"Thank you. Listen, I'm struggling to speak, need to save my strength. I'll pass you over to someone else now." I looked at Val for confirmation, she looked surprised, but after a thought nodded to me in agreement. "You must do everything she asks of you Mary. I have agreed to all of her demands. Please, do everything above board."

"Okay Sam. We will." Before passing the receiver over to Val, I had to ask: -

"*We?*"

"Yes, we. Your old friend Zoltan is here in London, with one of his daughters. He got in touch, oh, a day or so after you returned from France. He was asking all about you and insisted on coming over to see you in person. Anyway, he's here."

"Thanks Mary. That's good news." Val gave me a kick to the shin, prompting me to finish what she perceived as small talk and hand her the receiver. "Alright, got to go. Remember, give her whatever she wants Mary. No messing about. I need medical attention. Tell Zoltan I'm glad he's here, ask him to prepare field dressings for shotgun wounds..."

"What! You've been shot? Who shot you? How bad are you hurt? Sam what on Earth has happened to you?" Mary interrupted, her pitch rising, filled with alarm and concern.

"Only flesh wounds Mary, but deep. For now, I'm not so bad but I've lost close to a pint of blood already. I need you Mary, more than ever. I'm sorry to have to involve you, but there's nothing else I can think of. If we play along, I'll be fine. You can get hereabouts in a couple of hours on empty roads from central London. Be as quick as you can. I'll see you later." Val snatched the receiver from me.

"Mary, is it?" She barked down the mouthpiece, causing me to flinch.

"It is." Mary's voice, tinny and distant, crackled from the earpiece Val held close to her head.

"Right, listen. You may know this person as Sam, but I don't. I knew him as Dan. But all I want to know from you is has he got what he says he has. He told me he owns a haulage firm, is that right?"

"That is true yes. Well, no. Actually, he owns two."

"Does he now? And where are these firms based?"

"One is in Stoke, the other is in Cheshire."

"Are they? Now that is very interesting. And have you got access to the documents of ownership for these firms? You see, for Sam to live, I shall need those being put in my name, tonight. In a legal and binding way, mind."

"I do yes. I can get them from the safe in the office and bring them to you, wherever you want to meet."

"You can bring them here. I think we should be civilised about this. You will have to. I can't move him."

"How badly hurt is Sam exactly?' Mary asked, concern catching in her throat and peppering her syllables.

"Oh, don't worry, he'll live, long enough. You don't know much more about him than I do, do you?" Val's question came as more of an assertion but Mary answered it anyway.

"Probably not, no."

"Can you get to his gold?" Val asked, sticking to the point.

"His gold? What gold? Oh, the gold bullion he has in his deposit box at Coutts? No, I won't be able to get that. Even asking would raise eyebrows, and questions too. Coutts is a very private and exclusive bank." Mild confusion now lay in the tone of Mary's response. Val cupped the mouthpiece of the telephone's receiver and turned to me; -

"Oi! She says she can't get your gold out. She also said you own not one but two haulage firms, is that right?"

"Yeah. If Mary says it, it's true. Take them both. Worth more than the gold anyway."

"But what exactly do you own, as owner of the business?"

"Both firms have a fleet of trucks. Both are based on property I rent from local councils. I own the trucks, the machinery in the repair shops and anything else not nailed down there, as far as I know. The trucks alone are worth over a quarter of a million. Owning both businesses will set you up for life." Speaking took the wind from me and I had to slump back down to the floor as Val got back to Mary. The voices and words tumbled over beyond my comprehension, as debilitating fatigue swept over me once more. My head swam with thoughts I could not catch. Everything became vague. Despite remaining awake, the details of the conversation eluded me. Certain parts filtered through which seemed most pertinent. Val asked a lot of questions. From what I could perceive, Mary's answers satisfied Val enough to go ahead with my proposal. Mary asked Val for her number and arrangements were made for her to call Val once she had everything. The talk drifted on and on, leaving me far behind. Being unable to keep up. At one point, Val turned and looked me up and down with great deliberation. Her words were indecipherable as my awareness had slipped into a misty perplexity. Later it dawned on me that this had been in response to Mary's questions about my condition. I succumbed to fatigue and fell unconscious.

SALVATION SANS
REDEMPTION

"Wakey wakey Sam, your friends will be here soon", Val said. Her tone light and approachable. Did she really just say those words, in that manner? Stirring awake, the first sensation being a dry tongue. I tried to lick my lips but my mouth felt sticky with a burning, tasteless thirst. "Here I'll get you some water." Before I'd processed these words, Val held my head still whilst tipping a cool glass of water to my mouth. Wetting my lips enough to drink properly first, I took most of the glassful down with Val's help. "That better? She said, still sounding unhostile. Friendly, concerned even. What had happened?

"Thanks Val." My voice never sounded so feeble. "Where are we?" Propped up against a stack of pillows, I lay in the corner of an unfamiliar barn-like room, heavy brushes and other outdoor implements leaning against the corners. The place reminded me of a feed store in the stable-yard where I learned to ride in my youth. Stacks of wooden boxes were piled against the longer wall on my right. An old iron paraffin heater stood in the middle of the room, blasting out heat. At least three blankets were pulled around me and I lay atop an old wax greatcoat. This had been placed upon the remains of a hay bale, which Val had evidently put there and cut open, placing me on top wrapped in the coat and allowing me to sink into the hay, forming a bed of sorts.

"This is one of my outhouses Dan, I mean Sam. Fuck's sake you are an enigma, aren't you? Your secretary or whatever she is, Mary, she made me promise to do all I could to make you comfortable. She told me a lot about you Sam. Your friend Zoltan did too. Lived quite a life, haven't you?"

"Zoltan spoke to you?"

"Yes, he told me plenty. According to him you're a very special person Sam Daniels. I'm inclined to agree, but perhaps not for the same reasons." Val sat on a small barrel, a Firkin, lit the predictable cigarette and sat looking across at me. Knowing she had more to say, I remained quiet and waited for it. "You need to thank these friends of yours, they're good people. Without them things would be a lot different. But your right about one thing. With you dead I'd never have any peace. Sean's gone; nothing can ever change that. You killed him and now, I know why. You're insane Sam. Unhinged. But not entirely, and not incurably. Most of you is rational. You just need to be aimed in the right direction and have the right people around you. Whatever led a man in your position to pretend to be someone else, just so you could come round here to have it off with me, is something I'm struggling to understand."

"It weren't just that Val", I protested.

"Don't matter to me either way now. Don't worry about it. Whilst you've been asleep, I've not only been cleaning you up and sorting this place out for you. I've been thinking. And the only reason that I can think of, the only way it makes sense to me, is if you were running away from someone. And that someone could only be yourself. You were trying to avoid your impulses to kill. Like you told me, it went fine until that day when Sean walked in on us. The way he spoke to you, well, he's like that with everyone, especially anyone he doesn't know. But I can see how it set off a time bomb in you. He even said whilst you were there, didn't he? That very day the pair of you met, he said I'd only ever get this place over his dead body. Words to that effect anyway. You even joked about it if I remember right. He didn't like that." I nodded.

"When will they get here?" Asking to change the subject. Val's casual references to my murderous ways and slaying of her brother were unnerving. A twinge of recognition went through me at a very profound level. Some latent psychotic gene stirred in Val. Best move the conversation on to current affairs.

"Shouldn't be too long now, another half hour or so. You keep still and save your strength. I've stopped all your bleeding but haven't much to dress those wounds with properly. Zoltan said he'll be able to take care of it until they can get you to some private clinic, you're a member of?" Val's voice rose in pitch with this question, so I answered as best as I could.

"Yeah, it's down South, in Surrey. Mary must have told him about it."

"Won't take more than a few hours to get you down there then. You'll be alright." Shifting around still hurt like hell, but the lack of wetness testified to Val's assertions. She'd covered the wounded areas with bar towels. These had soaked up blood and now stuck to me as it had congealed. Any movement tugged at these and re-opened a few, but only drips of fresh blood formed. Val watched as I inspected her work and said; "Funnily enough the rock salt has helped keep the wounds clean."

"Yeah, probably why it stings like a bastard too."

"You feel better now though? A lot better than before, eh?" I rubbed my head, fingers instantly finding the sore lumps and bumps under my hair.

"I'm sore all over, but my head is clear enough now. The sleep did me good. So, you're ok with them coming here, to your place?"

"No other way to do it really is there Sam? We might as well be civilised and do this properly. As long as I end up the legal owner of those two haulage firms, I'm ok."

"You will be. Don't feel the need for the shotgun then?" I said, nodding at her.

"Now why would I need that, Sam? I'm not angry anymore and your friends sound genuine to me. Besides, I have this." Val reached inside the short jacket she wore and pulled out my Browning pistol. She had the bloody holster on too! "Just in case." Val winked, before re-holstering the gun and patting her jacket back into place. "I took the liberty of searching your Austin. I'll keep the keys, and the car too, along with your Wolsley, thanks. Nice pair of motors." She smiled, although in a warm way. I'd never witnessed this sense of humour in Val before, yet much of her life I knew very little about. She certainly was a most resourceful character.

"You don't need the gun Val."

"Let's hope not." Is all she said. Then; - "You feel up to a cup of tea? Should do you some good and bring you round a bit more for when your friends get here."

"Yeah, go on. A warm drink would be nice Val, thanks." She walked out and returned a few minutes later with the tea, and another for herself.

"OK, these documents of ownership, what are they exactly? How will I know if they're genuine or not?"

"I don't think Mary will have had time to produce forgeries Val." She merely shrugged, indicating for me to continue. "Tax returns are proof, and as I'm the sole share-holder, a document called the Articles of Organisation acts as proof of ownership in both cases. All we need do is change the name from mine to yours. Mary will draft up some form of receipt."

"But what if someone asks how much I paid for them?"

"Like who?"

"The tax-man for a start."

"You don't have to tell anyone anything. Tell them you won them in a game of poker. I don't care. There'll be no repercussions Val. After this is settled, you'll never hear from me again."

"Aww, come on now, don't be like that Dan, I mean Sam. Fucking hell I did it again. Fucking Dan Turner!" She wiped her mouth with the back of her hand as if wiping poison from her lips. "I still fucking hate that name, but don't worry, I've stopped hating you now." She paused, and we shared a look of great understanding, which still baffles me to this day. Val quickly turned away as if unconcerned and went on; - "Anyway, sorry for swearing. You know how I get when something irks me. But really, there's no need to be like that, Sam. We don't need to be friends but if this is to be legal and binding, we don't need to break contact altogether now either, do we?" What if there's complications?"

"What kind?" I asked.

"Your people on the ground at these haulage firms aren't going to be happy being told out of the blue they now have to get used to having me as a boss. No chance. I know what folk are like." Val paused again, this time to take out and light the inevitable cigarette.

She went on; - "Mary told me how she deals with all the paperwork and legal correspondence concerning your businesses. I don't know how to do all that stuff. There will have to be a changeover period Sam. But there's no need for you to be involved. Let me have use of Mary's know-how, until she can help find me a replacement, and to keep these businesses afloat until I've got a grip of them. I want to know how they run, from top to bottom, if I'm going to own them. We need to keep all the drivers on board, not to mention the customers. No point me getting these two firms if they both go bust within a year or two."

"Okay Val, no problem."

"Good. Now, rest up, I'll go and keep an eye out for your friend's car, they can't be too far away."

"Well, well, here he is. How are you Sam my friend? Just a flesh wound, eh?" Zoltan's infectious charm broke into the room like a beam of sunlight let into a dark, dusty barn upon the opening of its doors. The contemplation encompassing my mind for the previous few minutes blasted into extinction by my old friend's teasing. He came in sat on a wheelchair pushed by a young woman whose age looked to be late twenties. Despite her attire being crafted of a practical cut and style, her figure pushed out and curved inwards in perfect proportions, creating base, carnal allure without ostensible effort. Raven hair tied back into a plaited pony-tail, with a serious look in her green eyes and lacking a smile of any description. Despite this, she remained beautiful. However, before I could respond to Zoltan or be introduced to the enigmatic young woman, Mary's sweet tones reached my ears.

"Sam, Sam, we're here now. Oh, thank the lord we made it, what a journey! She drove so fast! Anyway, how're you feeling? We've got some medical stuff here to sort you out. We'll get you ready for travel and organise these business arrangements with Val, then get you off for some proper care.' Mary spoke these words whilst fussing over me, after bustling her way forward in the now crowded room.

Mary turned to Val, who stood in the open doorway. "Are we alright to start re-dressing these wounds right away, before we get down to business?" Val shrugged;

"Of course, go ahead. Are those the documents?" She asked, pointing to a sleek red leather briefcase of mine Mary carried. The thing had been loitering around a bottom drawer in my office filing cabinet for many months. A gift from a beneficiary of my investments, the owner of a firm of solicitors based in Cambridge. My initials stamped in embossed yet discreet gold letters across the middle of it, in a beautiful handwritten script. Despite these qualities, I'd never really taken to the case and had forgotten about it. Seeing it in Mary's hand in such incongruous circumstances and setting felt surreal. The thing captivated my attention. As if making the entire scenario a dream. I wished for a minute I was asleep. Things would be easier. All I need do is wake up.

"Sam, this is my eldest daughter, Tempeste. She has been looking forward to meeting you." Zoltan boomed these words from his chair, now stationary, to my right, yanking my mind from its reverie. Perhaps the blood loss affected my perceptions but the red briefcase seemed to take up the entire room for a moment. It did hold my only lifeline after all. Being unable to either stand or even sit up to greet her properly, Tempeste leaned forward and grasped my right hand, pulling it towards her and clasping my hand with both of her own, in the process jerking me forward and re-lighting the fires of pain along my left side.

"Bonsoir, Monsieur Daniels." Her tone low and delivery unemotional.

"Glad to meet you at last Tempeste," I said through the grimace. She let go of my hand showing no sign of concern for my pain but a puzzled look crossed her brow and she tilted her head at me.

"Your father used to talk about you when you were a little girl. He always spoke of you in the evenings." I told her.

"That's right" Zoltan said. "And what did I tell you?" He asked me but looked at his daughter.

I spoke to Zoltan but kept eye contact with Tempeste. "You used to tell me how she was going to be the best female soldier, no, an assassin. Yes, she was going to be the next Black Widow of France."

"Voila!" Zoltan exclaimed, giving Tempeste a triumphant look. She took a step back and allowed Mary to get close. Between them she and Zoltan refreshed my dressings and cleaned the wounds. Zoltan also gave me a couple of different tablets. "One for pain, one for fatigue. These will keep you going." Val produced a tray of drinks and I washed the pills down with hot, sweet tea. Within minutes I felt revived and refreshed. Whatever constituted those little tablets had incredible potency. Doubtful they were medically legal in the UK. Tempeste noticed this little exchange between myself and her father and made no bones about making sure he knew she had. Albeit without uttering a word nor even clearing her throat. The armour-penetrating powers of her gaze were more than enough. She flicked her eyes at me after I'd downed the pills and studied me for some seconds. When satisfied, she planted her gaze firmly back onto Zoltan. He kept himself turned away from her. I looked at her eyes but Tempeste ignored me. For certain the pair were in disagreement about Zoltan's prescription for my condition. I turned to Mary;

"Have you got everything Val needs then Mary?"

"Yes. Well, at least paperwork-wise." She answered. However, before I could respond, Val broke in.

"What do you mean? I hope you haven't been conning me all this time!" Mary smiled at her; -

"Of course not Val. There are things like spare sets of keys for company vehicles and some of the office buildings kept in a business safe Sam has in a London bank. I couldn't get them without Sam. You will need them if you're going to be showing your presence at your new businesses." Val smiled back at her and blinked, a little chagrined for raising her voice. "I can see why Sam kept you on so long." Mary shrugged.

"He wouldn't know what to do without me." Mary grinned at Val and they both laughed. The lack of hostility in the room became more palpable by the minute.

"She's right", I injected. "I forgot all about those keys!"

"He needs you all right Mary, that's for sure." Zoltan offered, his accented voice humorous and warm. He put his hand out to me. "Here, Sam, you get in my chair, I can manage on my wooden legs.

For the first time I noticed a pair of crutches by the door as Zoltan gestured towards them. The old wooden frame type. Mary or Val must have carried them over from the car. I looked at his chair, then at Tempeste, who gave me a curt nod. Zoltan followed this and said, "Don't worry, Tempeste will make sure to get you where you need to be. She will drive us back down South." I looked at Val, she and Mary were engrossed, poring over the documents. Mary gave Val a diamond studded platinum pen, crafted in Lichtenstein for her thirtieth birthday at my willing expense, to sign the paperwork with, then insisted Val keep the pen for herself. My world had flipped on its head. I wondered if the pills Zoltan gave me might have had a hallucinogenic effect on my addled senses. How had it all turned out so calm and proper? Not that I saw any reason to complain. The pair of them went about their business with striking efficacy. Before the events could register on my sense, Tempeste had wheeled me outside and shuffled me onto the spacious rear seat of a Mark I Range Rover, still in immaculate condition. Val right beside us, even helping fold the wheelchair and put in the back. Tempeste jumped behind the wheel, Mary got in the back with me. Zoltan made his way to the open passenger door after waving further help from Tempeste away, then he stood holding the door for support and beckoned Val over to him.

"Please, no need to say anything Valerie." Again, no sense or logic could be attributed to this from my brain. Somehow the way Zoltan said those words with his thick accent and gruff tones made them reminiscent of the famous quote attributed to Napoleon Bonaparte – *"Not tonight, Josephine…"* As surreal as these occurrences were, my senses were heightened by this point due to the pills I'd took.

Val walked over and stood on the other side of the door from him. Zoltan chuckled, causing Val to smile with genuine warmth. "I never told Sam that holster you are wearing was made to fit our Tempeste here, but she had lost the need to carry small arms before we could give it to her, such is her passion for her work." Prompted by this, Tempeste turned around to smile at Mary and I, albeit only a little, without showing her teeth. Now though, her eyes lit up. Val went to reply to Zoltan, then held herself steady. Surprised and irritated that he'd discerned she had the Browning. Zoltan huffed.

"Forget about it, we all need a little security, no? Besides, what's done is done, yes? Like we agreed on the phone, no?" Val raised her eyebrows at Zoltan's verbiage, smiled at him and nodded her agreement. "Here, take this." Zoltan went on, reaching out and placing something in Val's hands.

"What is this?" Val asked, without looking down. Answering her own question by opening the envelope Zoltan had handed to her and fanning out a thick wad of twenty-pound notes. "How much is here?" Val's voice rising in surprise. She looked at me, I shrugged and shook my head. Zoltan looked at Mary; -

"How much was it exactly, Mary?"

"Six thousand, seven hundred and thirty. There's a single tenner in the middle, to help you find it. Mary smiled her sweet, genuine smile at Val once again.

"So I see," Val replied, whilst still holding the money fanned out held towards us, she asked; -

"But what's it for?"

"It is for you." Zoltan answered, reaching into the glove box. "So is this." He passed her another envelope. This one larger, buff coloured and with a little ribbon-tie to hold it shut. Before he could make a move to pass it to her though, Val spoke up.

"Listen, I don't want to owe anyone any money. This is more than we arranged."

"Relax", Zoltan soothed her, "Think of it as a guarantee, a transition fee if you like."

"It's all the cash Sam had in his office safe, along with those documents you needed Val." Mary said.

"So, what are those, then?" Val answered, pointing at the larger envelope Zoltan had tried handing to her, still clutched in his left hand before her.

"Canadian Bail Bonds. Around eight, nine thousand," he looked over at Tempeste who nodded her assertion, "Eight, nine thousand in English pounds, although these are in Canadian Francs. But do not worry, they are easily exchanged. We bought them over with us, for some other business. This is more important. They are yours now." He stretched out and waved them in front of Val to take. She did.

"Any problems, you have my home number and the office number is on those notes I left with the rest of the paperwork Val. Don't hesitate to give me a ring if you need me." Mary said, rolling the car window down to reach out to hold hands with Val. Tempeste manoeuvred the Range rover around the yard as Val opened the gate. She smiled, then waved at us. We sped off into what remained of the night.

Two of a Kind

"What brings you to England then Zoltan?" I asked as we negotiated the bumpy back lanes leading away from Val's place. The combined effects of Zoltan's medication and the off-road suspension of the Range Rover mercifully saving me from too much pain.

"I came for you of course! This is why we are here, for you. Even before all this craziness that has happened today. No, no, we are here to save you from yourself Sam Daniels. Tempeste here has things to tell you."

"Oh, really? What things?" Confusion swept my thoughts. Mary squeezed my hand; -

"There really is too much to talk about right now Sam, you need to rest", she said.

"I need to know! None of this makes sense to me, how come Val was being so nice? What did you tell her on the 'phone?" My protest surprised me with its vigour.

"I only told Val what Tempeste had already told me Sam. Then she had to hear it from Tempeste herself", Zoltan replied, turning to me and reaching to touch my leg with earnestness. "It is Tempeste who knew all that Val needed to hear."

"And what was that?" My question resonated within the car for a few seconds, diminishing into the thrum of the engine and drone of the tyres on the road. Evidently Zoltan felt Tempeste should answer me. She waited a minute or so until we turned onto a larger, straighter road. Then after adjusting the rear-view mirror in order to be able to make eye contact with me when she could, Tempeste elucidated.

"Val's brother was doomed already Sam, make no mistake", Zoltan's arduous daughter began telling me. "The Turkish gang he worked for were going to set him up next time he went over there. It is what they do, they have done it many times to their couriers from other countries. Once they have made their own connections, that's it. He would have ended up dead anyway, within a year. And Val would never have known whether he still lived or not. His body would not have been found." Tempeste paused as she negotiated slower traffic. "Either dead or in a Turkish jail for the rest of his life. And that is a fate worse than death. Those places are hell on Earth for foreigners, especially westerners. You may have murdered him, but ultimately you saved him." Despite the message being so profound, I marvelled at how Tempeste could speak English with little of her French accent coming through. Only one question flashed like a neon sign in my mind's eye.

"How do you know all of this?" Zoltan answered for his formidable offspring; -

"Tempeste is a senior officer for Interpol Sam, they have been tracking the Turkish gangs smuggling heroin throughout Europe for some time. Cornering them in England is easier than most places, so when an English connection showed up, they followed him. An undercover operative of theirs's had connection with the same gang that came over here to England with Val's brother."

"Sean", I spoke.

"Yes, Sean Frobisher." Tempeste responded. "What made you kill him?"

"It's a long story." Swerving further inquiry, I asked; "So you told all this to Val and she accepted it?"

"She felt the truth of it. Val knew Sean was in far above his head anyway, and that sooner or later he would get himself into something he could not get out of. That is what she told me", Tempeste asserted. Something about her, some *gravitas* Tempeste held, made it evident she spoke with certainty. Qualities Val would no doubt have felt herself. Tempeste convinced you with her aura and self-assurance, as much as her words. "I came here after Papa spoke to me about you. When you bought the gun off him, you mentioned a Turkish gang of heroin smugglers. Papa was concerned about you and mentioned it to me, to see if I might be able to help in some way. Obviously, you did not need any help." At this Zoltan spoke up; -

"My concern was how you'd gotten into such a mess in the first place Sam. You were not yourself when you came to me for that gun. I could tell something had been bothering you for some time."

"If only you knew." My words soft, distant.

"But we do not need to know Sam. No-one does. Keep your bad days to yourself, better that way. Maybe one day you can write a book and tell us all about it."

"Maybe I will do just that Zoltan, when I'm really old. Only if I outlive Val though. If I'm going to put it all in print, there's stuff she never needs to know." He gave a short, well-informed laugh, nodding to himself. Next, without looking over but by gesturing with his head, Zoltan got to the point. "Look, Sam. Tempeste has come over to help you, to make you an offer. Maybe it will be best if you accept her offer. Work with her, with her people." He answered.

"Make me an offer?" Intrigue gripped me, pushing the pains and discomforts still further down. Zoltan shrugged.

"Interpol has a covert, secret element. An international extermination service, if you like. Very secret. Very professional. To take care of any individuals whose activities create problems affecting several governments at one time. People who have a way of remaining beyond the obvious reach of the law, if you understand me, Sam?" He did not turn around to register my response. He knew I understood him clearly. "There will be, opportunities, for you to do those things you do so well. But do not misunderstand me, no-one is here to judge you for whatever you did to bring you to this point. Such things can only be decided between you and your maker. I know you Sam, remember? How wild you were in Africa?" He laughed, turning to look at me for a second. "And how many times did you save the day? How many times did you save my life? I for one know how good you are at what you do best, let us leave it at that. Just as I also know how good my beautiful Tempeste here is at what *she* does best. Same as you Sam, same as you." His last words grew fainter as he turned to look out the passenger window. With a heavy sigh, he stared out in silence, as if looking across into the distance. As did Mary. Although beyond the glass, the dark of night obscured all details from their view.

The End

Printed and bound by CPI Group (UK) Ltd, Croydon, CR0 4YY